FRIENDS
OF ACPL

W9-CMT-762

3 1833 00

ONE SUMMER IN STOCK

Books by Kathleen S. Tiffany

MARY FLORENCE,
The Little Girl Who Knew Abraham Lincoln

ONE SUMMER IN STOCK

KATHLEEN S. TIFFANY

One Summer

in Stock

DODD, MEAD & COMPANY

NEW YORK —— 1957

© 1957 by Kathleen S. Tiffany
All rights reserved

No part of this book may be reproduced in any form
without permission in writing from the publisher

Library of Congress Catalog Card Number: 57-6036

Printed in the United States of America
by The Cornwall Press, Inc., Cornwall, N. Y.

U. S. 980024

To Susan—who loves "theater"

Contents

The characters and situations in this book are wholly fictional and imaginative: they do not portray and are not intended to portray any actual persons or parties.

1

A Growing Doubt

THEY HADN'T TALKED MUCH on the way from the movie to the Snak Bar. Now, seated two by two across the small table in the booth, Betty sighed in contentment.

"Ooh!" she exclaimed. "Wasn't it wonderful? I'm crazy about Ronald Birch. He's dreamy."

Betty's date, Jim, gave an impatient shrug.

"I don't see what you girls go so crazy over in these movie characters."

"Didn't you like it?" Betty asked.

"Sure—it was O.K., I guess." Jim sounded uncertain and Nan, watching and listening, knew that he was only disturbed by Betty's admiration for the actor, not by the very stupid picture they'd just seen.

She looked across the table at Pete, her own date, and asked directly, "Pete, what did you think of the movie?"

"I thought it was swell. Why?"

Oh, dear, Nan thought, I might have known! Why did I ask? Honesty compelled her to answer.

"Well, I thought it was dull. The plot was stereotyped and the acting was awful."

Pete looked at her and there was anger in his voice when he retorted, "Look, I've been home from college for two weeks and we've had three dates for the movies and you haven't liked any of them. Does that fancy drama school of yours teach you to look down on everything?"

"No, it doesn't. It just happens that it does give me some discrimination. Besides, I told you I liked the way some of the parts were acted in the other two movies. This one was just pretty bad all the way through."

Pete drummed his fingers on the table top and seemed about to reply when Betty cut in, "Oh, let's not fight about an old movie. Who cares anyway? What are you going to have? I want a hot fudge, nut sundae."

"I'll take the Supreme Special," Jim said.

Pete took a little longer to decide, but by the time the waitress came over he had chosen a banana split.

The three orders were given and then Pete asked, "What about you, Nan?"

"I'll take a large coke, with cherry."

Once more Pete sounded angry. "Oh, come on. Order something good."

"That's all I want," Nan assured him; so it was ordered. Nan knew, however, that Pete was aware of how much she loved sweets and that her order had been given simply because she was determined not to put on weight, or to spoil her complexion, so she understood him perfectly when he said, "Nan, I wish you'd give the whole thing up. Why don't you go to business school, if you don't want college?"

"Or you could get a job. My firm hires girls all the time. I could put a word in for you," Jim offered.

"Thanks," Nan said, and her voice was perilously close to shaking. "Mother and I decided I'd go to drama school. I like it. Can't you leave me alone?"

"If you really want to do it yourself, O.K.," Pete said. "But if it's just because your mother wants you to, I wish you'd quit. You haven't been the same since, and that's a fact."

Nan knew it was so, but with an effort at firmness she replied, "Well I want to—so, let's change the subject."

The subject was duly changed and the rest of the afternoon passed pleasantly.

Nan remembered all this two days later, when she dropped the phone receiver onto its hook with a little jerk that was like a slap. Angry tears filled her eyes as she went back to her room to continue dressing.

"It isn't as if he didn't *know*. I already *told* him I'd be busy this evening—"

Her mother's voice came from the adjoining bedroom. "Who was it, Nan?"

"Just Pete," she answered and did not tell her mother that he had asked her to go out and that, when she had explained why she couldn't go, he had been—so—well, *nasty*, was the word for it.

Nan and Pete had dated during his last year in high school. When he had gone off to college, and she had entered as a student at the Booth Theater School and Workshop, they had written to one another, and whenever he was in town, he had always taken her out.

More and more often, though, due to the Booth Stock Company, in which she now and again had a small part, Nan had been forced to refuse Pete's offers of a date. So far, he had taken it pretty well, but tonight he had not. He wouldn't even *try* to understand that she was obligated to go tonight. All the students were.

Ever since Nan had been a small child, she had loved the theater and everything connected with it. When she was still a youngster in grade school, her mother had taken her to many of the best Broadway plays for Saturday matinees and gradually Nan had begun to think she might become an actress when she grew up.

At first she had acted solely for her own pleasure; before a mirror at home, or dancing dreamily to the record player, but after she entered high school she had regularly tried out for all the school plays and generally received good parts.

It was true that none of her close friends were interested in the theater, but surely Pete had known for long enough how she felt. The only difference was that now she *was* more critical and often couldn't help showing it.

In honesty she had to admit that she was bothered by the gradual loosening of ties between herself and her high school friends. Her hours, her interests, were no longer the same as theirs. Pete had just brought it to a head, but Nan did wish that he had not suggested that the whole idea of drama school was her mother's and not her own. It wasn't really—or was it?

Subtly her anger turned from Pete to the school. It did seem silly that even the first-year students were expected to attend the graduation. Why?

"Darn it!" The exclamation was torn from her as, in her angry mood, the zipper on her new dress caught when she jerked it up.

"What's the matter, dear?" her mother asked, coming into the room.

"The old zipper!" Nan said and tugged at it wilfully.

"Here—let me—you'll only make it worse." Mrs. Lane bent to help and suddenly Nan's anger left her. Mother was so lovely and she wanted this career for her daughter so badly. Nan couldn't bear to let her know what was troubling her.

Mrs. Lane, working slowly and carefully to disengage

the cloth, said, "I knew this color would be just right for you when I saw the dress."

Nan looked over her mother's bent head to the mirror on the dresser. Reflected there she saw a girl in a turquoise dress, with auburn hair, gray eyes and a wide mouth, set now in sullenness. Nan took a cautious breath and smiled, deliberately, at her image.

"It's lovely, Mother," she declared.

"There!" The zipper was loose. Mrs. Lane slipped it up and straightened to take Nan's face between her hands and kiss it.

"I'm all excited over this evening," she said, then added, "We'd better hurry, though, or we'll be late. Your grandmother is ready."

"It won't take me a minute now to brush my hair," Nan told her. Mrs. Lane nodded and left the room.

Nan took up her hairbrush and vigorously stroked the waving auburn hair, so like her mother's.

What had she really been angry about? Pete's threat that he was through with her? Yes—but it had been her pride that was hurt. She didn't really *care* for Pete, she was beginning to realize.

Ever since his return from college for the summer she had known that he meant less to her than he once had. He seemed so self-centered, and yes, childish.

He was two years older than she, but at nineteen he seemed to be satisfied to do and say the same things he had done and said in high school.

The issue of the movies was only a small part of the change that had taken place between them. It wasn't the theater itself that made the difference. It was that the theater people were so much more mature and she had gotten used to that during this past year.

At first she had felt really lost without her old crowd, but, though she was almost the youngest of the students at her drama school, she had come to enjoy their company.

They *thought* about so many things and discussed them, too.

Then there was very little dating, as such, among them. They were all too absorbed in their work. This didn't seem to make them nervous, though, as she had known girls to be nervous in high school if they didn't have a date.

Anyway, she decided, she would stop thinking about Pete now. She had a feeling that, if she *really* wanted to win him back, she could. It gave her a comforting sense of power.

Nan rose from the dresser, put on her hat and coat and joined her mother and grandmother for the trip downtown.

2

Graduation Night

THE MINGLED ODOR of grease paint and dust that Nan had become used to in the small auditorium was missing tonight. In its place there was the heavy scent of flowers and perfume.

Jack Fenton, one of the second-year students, was at the door, taking tickets, and he smiled at Nan as she came in with her mother and grandmother.

"Good evening, Mrs. Lane," he said formally to Nan's mother. "There are two seats right over here." To Nan, in a lower voice, he added, "Reminds me of my high-school graduation!"

Nan laughed. "I'll seat them, Jack," she said, and, leaving him to greet the next people to come in, she led her mother and grandmother over to the seats he had indicated.

Already the small auditorium was half filled and here and there Nan recognized the parents of other pupils of the Booth Theater School and Workshop.

"I'll leave you, Mother," Nan said, as they reached the two empty seats. "I do hope you'll enjoy it."

"You know I will! Just think, not so long from now you'll be graduating and really starting your career."

Nan felt that her mother was more excited than she was.

7

"I hope you like it, too, Grandma," she said, more to avoid answering her mother directly than anything else.

"It won't be the first graduation I've seen, nor the last, I hope, and I always enjoy them. Who was that nice-looking young man that spoke to us at the door, Nan?"

Mrs. Lane frowned and Nan giggled. Grandmother and mother—what a pair they were! And she loved both of them so much.

Mother wanted Nan to have a career in the theater. Grandmother wanted to see Nan married young. Sometimes, Nan felt, if they would leave her alone, she might have a chance to discover for herself what *she* wanted.

"That was Jack Fenton, Grandmother, and he's engaged to the pretty dark girl over there to the extreme right of the front row."

Grandmother looked over and, after having considered the girl, said, decisively, "She's not a bit prettier than you are—"

"Now, Mother!" Mrs. Lane said warningly. The woman who was seated directly back of them smiled in amusement and Nan flushed scarlet.

"Be seeing you," she said and fled, grateful that tonight she had to sit with the other members of her class. They were the beginners' class and they were located down toward the front, on the left. Nan made her way there and sat down between her friend, Monica Leslie, and Mark Byron.

"What's the matter, Nan?" Monica asked. "You look awfully hot and flushed."

Nan laughed and the color began to recede from her fair skin.

"Me and my blushes!" she groaned disgustedly. "It was just Grandmother and Mother again. Mother can't *wait* till

I start my career and Grandmother hinted quite publicly
that Jack seemed an eligible young man for me! I could see
Mother was beginning to be annoyed at her, so I left. . . .
Honestly, Monica, families can be so embarrassing!"

"You can say that again," Monica agreed and both girls
fell silent, busy with their own thoughts.

"Look! Oh, Nan, do look!" Monica exclaimed suddenly.
"Over there, near the exit, with Mr. Lloyd. That's surely
Edith Trevor?"

Nan looked and sat up straighter, for it was indeed Edith
Trevor, deep in conversation with Mr. Lloyd, the director
of the school. Nan alerted Mark and he, too, gazed at the
distinguished pair.

"I heard that tonight there'd be lots of theater people
here—I mean for graduation night. Isn't she, well—"

"Magnificent!" Nan breathed and the phrase fitted. Dig-
nity, poise and true presence set the great actress apart, even
though she was dressed very simply and, at the moment,
was so absorbed in her conversation as to seem wholly
unaware of the impression she was making.

"Oh, look, there's Eric Welch," Nan told Monica, as a
tall, handsome man sat down to the right of them.

By now both girls were frankly craning their necks to
try and see who else of note might be in the audience—
and Nan had completely forgotten the beginning of her
evening. This was the magic of the theater world—the way
it blotted out time and all other events.

Nan, Monica and Mark were not alone in their interest.
The whole group of students was keenly aware of the presence of the luminaries of their world and down the rows of
seats the magic names of actors, actresses and critics flew
from one to another—except for the seniors. Those fortunate beings who, after tonight, would be a real part of the

world they had been trained for—or who, at least, would try now in earnest to enter that world. The seniors held aloof from whisperings and the turning of heads; yet Nan could tell by their very studied indifference how keyed up they were.

Beside her, Monica giggled.

"Look at Alicia," she whispered.

Nan looked and delightedly turned to Mark. Alicia Van Delyss was, of all the seniors, the most affected, conceited and "upstage." Talented, yes, but merciless toward others. Sure of her own destiny she was, at times, downright ruthless with the lesser fry. No one liked her, not even her classmates. Yet everyone conceded her amazing talent. Right now, she was standing up in the aisle. Her thick black hair was combed straight back and coiled in a massive knot low on her neck. Her features were almost classically perfect; her eyes almond shaped and of a peculiar hazel color. "Like a cat's eyes," someone had said once—and they were.

Mark followed the direction of Nan's whispered comment and nodded.

"What do you bet she's going to try and talk to Miss Trevor?" he asked.

"No doubt about it. Right now, though, she's trying to be seen first."

So absorbed was Nan in the little drama being played out by Alicia that a tap on her own shoulder startled her. Turning, she found her mother leaning over the aisle seat in back of her and beckoning.

Reluctantly, Nan edged past Mark's knees and joined her mother, who took her by the elbow and, talking in a low tone, started for the back of the auditorium.

It took a few moments for the sense of what was being said to her to penetrate Nan's understanding.

"—So," she heard her mother say, "he told me he knew Miss Trevor well and he would be glad to introduce you and I *knew* what a thrill it would give you, so—"

Nan stopped in panic. "Oh, Mother, no!"

"Now, Nan, don't be ridiculous. I've already asked him. He'll just introduce us. It never hurts in the theater—*or* in the newspaper business, for that matter, to know the right people."

Nan knew that her mother was right and it certainly wasn't that she didn't *want* to meet Miss Trevor. It was just that she had been making fun of Alicia, and also—she was plain scared. Yet, she couldn't very well create a scene, like a balky child. So, the telltale blush once more suffusing her face, she allowed her mother to lead her toward a tall, dinner-jacketed man.

"Harry, this is my aspiring Thespian, Nan. Nan, this is Mr. Woolock, the drama critic. We worked on the same paper some years ago."

Mr. Woolock shook hands formally with Nan and in an admiring tone said, "Looks a lot like you, Laura."

"Yes, we do look alike, I think."

"Same sparkle, same auburn hair, gray eyes— How about the dimples, do you have them, too?"

Nan smiled and they appeared. Mr. Woolock gave her shoulder a squeeze. "Don't be nervous. Miss Trevor won't bite, you know."

"Do I look that nervous?" Nan asked, alarmed.

"On you, it is becoming," he assured her and, taking mother and daughter by the arms, guided them toward Miss Trevor.

From that moment until Miss Trevor's cool fingers met hers in a firm handclasp, Nan was in a daze. The actress' well-known, husky voice greeted her warmly, though what she said Nan did not know.

Mr. Woolock saved the moment by saying bluntly, "The girl is scared to death, Edith."

The Trevor laugh was low, but kind, "Of course she is. Harry, it's rather unfair of you to use me in scaring the young. Tell me, are you graduating tonight?"

Nan found her voice. "Oh, no, Miss Trevor. I have two years still to go."

"Do you like it?"

"Yes, Miss Trevor, but—but, I'm not quite sure yet that I like it well enough to make a career of it . . . and I'm certainly not sure that I have the talent."

"Well it's best to be honest with yourself, my dear. You look very young?"

"Seventeen."

"These days that is young. You have time. The theater is a wonderfully satisfying world to those who love it; but it needs devotion—and there are other worlds. Some of my own family have longed for other worlds, but we were born and raised in the profession. Well, Harry, I'll see you after the graduation? Glad to have met you, Mrs. Lane— and, Nan, don't let *anyone* make up your mind for you."

There was something compelling in Miss Trevor's voice and Nan found herself replying with deep sincerity, "I won't, I promise."

The actress turned once more to Mr. Lloyd and together they made their way toward the stage. Nan and her mother and Mr. Woolock retraced their steps, but halfway up the aisle Alicia Van Delyss stepped directly in their path.

"Darling," she said, "you look wonderful tonight. This can't be your mother? She looks just like your sister."

Nan stared at the girl in amazement. As far as she could

remember, it was the one and only time that Alicia had spoken directly to her. Her innate good manners came to her rescue, however.

"Mother, this is Alicia Van Delyss. She is graduating to-night. May I present Mr. Woolock? Miss Van Delyss."

There was a brief exchange of greetings between Alicia and the others and then, as the house lights dimmed in warning, Nan found her way back to her seat.

"What happened? Who was the man who introduced you to Miss Trevor?" Monica whispered. "You should have seen Alicia's face. Was she burned up!"

"You lucky dog, what's she like?" Mark asked on the other side.

"*Shh!* Tell you later," Nan whispered back. The audience was quieting down now, the chatter dying away.

Onto the stage walked the faculty and Miss Trevor.

Nan sat back and sighed. The tension she had been under in meeting Miss Trevor, Alicia's queer behavior afterward, and even the excitement of Mark and Monica, had put her under a strain. She was glad now to be able to sit back and watch and listen.

3

A Door Opens

IT WASN'T UNTIL the speeches were well under way, however, that Nan put aside her preoccupation with all that had happened and began to really listen.

They were, like most graduation speeches, she thought, a blend of encouragement and hope for the future, and also of warning—warning that the future now belonged to the graduates, that it was up to them to make good—all of it spiced with suitable bits of humor, like sugar-coating on a pill.

Nan was so pleased with her own simile that she once more lost track of what the speakers were saying, until the time for awarding the diplomas came. This part of the ceremony was prefaced by a brief explanation from Mr. Lloyd, who said, in part, "In awarding these diplomas, we accord our graduates an equal share. We do not award grades for scholarship as do universities, colleges and lower schools. We say, most simply, this young person has been trained by us and by us is now considered fitted to enter professional life. That life will in its turn award you according to your merit. However, there are several of our graduates, who, whether through being seen here in the plays we produce during the season or in summer stock or,

14

in some cases, on Broadway, have already been offered contracts. These we shall mention as we hand out their diplomas. I explain this that you mày know that these young people are being rewarded in the life they have chosen, but also that you may know that these rewards do not come from the school itself. There is, however, one exception to this rule tonight. It is a new departure for us, as a school, and we thought long before accepting the offer it contained. We finally did this because the offer brings such a golden opportunity for one of the young people we have studying with us this year.

Now indeed Nan and her classmates were alert.

"The manager of the Murray Stock Company of Metropolis, Indiana, has offered to take one of our beginners for a season of stock at a nominal salary. It is really a training period. We have endeavored to reach a fair judgment in selecting this pupil, basing our decision not so much on achievement as on potentiality and attitude toward work. After the awarding of the diplomas, therefore, we will announce the winner of this special school scholarship."

Some one started to clap and a few others followed the example but were quickly quieted, as Mr. Lloyd raised his hand for silence, saying, "I know you have all recognized Miss Trevor on the platform." This time there was a really spontaneous outburst of applause in which Nan joined. When it quieted, Mr. Lloyd continued, "Miss Trevor has graciously consented to hand out our diplomas tonight. It gives me great pleasure to introduce Miss Edith Trevor."

Miss Trevor came forward and she and Mr. Lloyd shook hands as the applause broke out once more. She bowed to the audience and then walked over to the table where the diplomas lay. Someone in the audience called out, "Speech," and was promptly shushed. A rustling of people in the small hall betrayed the tension of pupils and parents alike and then the first name was called: "Arnold Abrahams."

From his place among the seniors, Arnold rose and walked up the steps onto the stage to receive his diploma and a shake of the hand from Edith Trevor.

Alphabetically the names were called. Jill Ames, Mr. Lloyd announced, had been signed for a small part in a forthcoming musical. There was a good deal of applause, for she was both popular and talented. Marvin Brett was signed for summer stock in Harford. More applause. The list went on and soon Alicia Van Delyss' name was called. A little murmur of approval came from the audience as she rose and made her way toward the stage.

She *looked* like an actress, Nan thought, and did not wonder that the audience reacted so. It did not occur to Nan then that Alicia looked far more like an actress, as actresses are visioned by the public, than did Miss Trevor.

The students had expected that Alicia would receive some professional offer and they were right, for it was announced that she had been signed by the Murray Stock Company.

"Pity the poor beginner who has to go 'on scholarship' with her in the company," Mark whispered and Nan smiled.

None of the pupils had said anything to the audience, but merely accepted their diplomas and murmured a "thank you" to Miss Trevor. But Alicia, on accepting her diploma, said quite clearly, "Thank you, Miss Trevor," and then, turning to the audience, added, "I hope I shall deserve your applause in the future."

Oddly enough, the applause she did receive was markedly less than for the others, who had preceded her, or so Nan thought.

The last to receive a diploma was Martin Wingate and, as there were no names beginning with X, Y, or Z in the school that year, Mr. Lloyd again stepped forward. He asked for and received thunderous applause for the whole graduating class, who stood up to receive it.

When the applause stopped he said, "We will now award the scholarship of which I spoke. With it go our best wishes to the pupil chosen and our thanks to the Murray Stock Company and its director, Mr. Stewart Murray." He paused and Nan looked quickly around her. Almost all her classmates were leaning forward tensely.

"The pupil whom we have chosen in faculty conference is Miss Nan Lane. Nan, will you stand up and come forward, please."

For a moment it did not register with Nan herself. Then she stood on shaking legs until Mark gently pushed her past him. Like a sleepwalker, she went slowly forward toward the stage and up the steps where Mr. Lloyd, perhaps sensing her fright, came forward and led her to Miss Trevor.

It was precisely at this moment that Nan remembered with devastating clarity what she had told Miss Trevor before the ceremony began. To her relief, Miss Trevor smiled at her warmly and, under cover of the applause, said, "This will give you that chance to make up your mind that you need, child. Do not think it wasted. No matter what you do, it is never wasted, if your attitude is right, and yours must be or you would not have been chosen. It is an open door. I like your honesty. Keep it."

The patter of handclapping decreased, perhaps because Miss Trevor was so plainly seen to be speaking, so Nan stammered her thanks and got back to her seat, still be-wildered.

Shortly afterward, the auditorium was abuzz with chatter and Nan was surrounded by her classmates, congratulating her. When she at last worked her way back to where her mother and grandmother sat, she found her mother dabbing at the tears of happiness in her shining eyes. They hugged each other and Mrs. Lane exclaimed triumphantly, "I knew it, Nan! I knew you had talent. Oh, dear, I expect such great things of you!"

Nan kissed her and said soberly, "I'll try my best, Mother."

"Of course you will, Nan," Grandmother chimed in, "You always were a good worker when you set your mind to it. Guess you can even work at talent and make a go of it, if that's what you want."

"Now, Mother—" Mrs. Lane began, but Nan cut her short.

"I know what you mean, Grandmother. I haven't half the talent, natural talent, of some of the others, but I do work—and this summer should help me to know if that is enough."

"God bless you, child," Grandmother said and kissed her in her turn.

As the trio went out into the night, Nan thought, "It's funny how I feel closer to Grandmother than Mother some-times, and yet Mother has given me everything I have and I'm so proud of her."

The three of them happily celebrated Nan's wonderful good luck by having dinner in a Chinese restaurant and then taking a cab home, an unaccustomed luxury, which made it fun.

Before she went to bed, Nan said, "Mother, I do hope

I'll be all you want me to be. I think I do have a certain amount of talent and I know I love the theater, but I've sometimes wondered if that is enough. Anyway, I'm going to try to find out this summer."

"I know you will, dear, and I'll do my best to give you all the preparation you need. I have high hopes and great confidence in you, you know."

"I'll try, Mother, really I will," Nan replied, and Mrs. Lane kissed her warmly before leaving the room.

Nan knew she would not be able to sleep after all she had experienced that evening. She lay awake for quite a while, turning over in her mind everything that the summer ahead would mean to her and to her mother.

Nan remembered what Miss Trevor had said—it was an "open door." A door which her own talent and effort had opened.

She knew that her moments of self-doubt were partly just being young and uncertain, but there was also, still lurking and undismissed, the possibility that perhaps she had never given another sort of life enough thought. She also knew how much this evening had meant to her mother and that too troubled her. It was as if she were two people. The first person thrilled by her chance, eager to make good; the second standing back and questioning. Could she make her mother understand?

Mrs. Lane had been both father and mother to Nan since the death of Nan's father when she was still a small child. Nan knew that her mother, brought up in a small town, had had no preparation for any other career than marriage. It was a testimony to her mother's intelligence and will that she had made a place for herself in the newspaper world.

The way had been hard. Starting as a reporter on a small

town paper, Mrs. Lane had moved on to a larger city. Now, at middle age, she was a feature writer on the woman's page of a large New York daily. Nan knew that her mother had almost an obsession about the early choosing of a career and the proper preparation for it. On the other hand, Nan could see that, for herself, a home and a family, should the right boy come along, would have an almost irresistible attraction.

As an only child, she had always envied those of her friends who had brothers and sisters; the larger the family, the more she was attracted to it. It was, however, pretty idle to daydream about marriage when she had not been asked! Nor could she think of a single boy of her acquaintance, and certainly not Pete, to whom she might say "yes." Nan laughed at herself, gave herself a mental shake and pledged that in the year ahead she would not think of anything but the theater.

Having decided this, she snuggled down in bed and went to sleep, thinking how nice it would be if Mark Byron were going to be nearby this summer. Of all the boys she had met, she liked him the best. It did not occur to her that this was an odd way to begin that sole devotion to the theater to which she had just pledged herself!

4

A Person Set Apart

NAN SLEPT SO SOUNDLY after the excitement and stimulus of graduation night that her mother had already left for work when she wakened and, still drowsy, walked back to the kitchen of the apartment. There she found her grandmother washing the breakfast dishes.

"Good morning," Nan yawned, stretched and looked at the clock. "My goodness! Is it really ten o'clock?"

"Ten o'clock it is and I'm glad you had a good sleep. What do you want for breakfast?"

"Oh, I'll get it, Grandmother. Don't you bother."

"It's no bother. Just you sit down. It won't be long before you won't be here to get breakfast for . . . Now, what do you want? Cereal? Eggs? Toast?"

"Juice. Bacon and eggs and toast. I'm hungry."

"Good! You can pour your own orange juice—it's ready in the icebox. Well, how do you feel about the scholarship this morning?"

"Funny," Nan answered. "I mean, it doesn't seem real —not like it did last night. It is real, though, isn't it?"

"Yes, it's real. I can't say that I approve of a girl your age going off alone with a bunch of actors and actresses. But then, I'm old-fashioned. Your mother tells me you'll be well looked after; that in some ways it is sort of like boarding school—without the lessons."

Nan smiled and then sobered.

"It's going to seem awfully strange, being away from home. Some way I never thought of it really happening till I was much older." She looked around the kitchen, from the worn linoleum to the crisp curtains at the window, and the row of struggling plants on the sill which were her grandmother's special care. Sighing with a foretaste of homesickness, she poured her orange juice, popped two slices of bread in the toaster and sat down at the white enamel-topped table while her grandmother busied herself at the gas range.

Suddenly Nan jumped up. "Grandmother!" she exclaimed, "Do you realize nobody knows about what's happened to me? I mean none of the crowd. Betty and Daisy and Dan and Pete—they don't even know!"

Her grandmother chuckled. "You can tell them the news after breakfast. Call them up. They'll live till then, I presume."

"Oh, Grandmother!" Nan said, for she knew she was being teased. But she sat down willingly, strangely reluctant to tell her news to her oldest friends, the boys and girls she had grown up with.

This summer, Nan had planned, as usual, to spend two weeks at the cottage in Stonington, where she and her mother boarded each summer, then to stay on at Betty's home when her mother returned to work—to swim, to dance, to sail, to loaf. What fun it had always been! For many years the same group had been together. This past year, even while busy with dramatic school, Nan had known that Pete was always there. Her boy friend! Nan had liked him a lot, liked his tall build, his fair good looks. He was a wonderful dancer, a good dresser and the other girls envied her his attention. Yet now that meant little to her. What did she want?

Nan felt a strong tendency to cry but shook it off and began to eat. Surprisingly, the food made her feel a great deal better. Finishing off her last bite of toast, and with her mouth still full, she asked, "Grandmother, do you really think I'll make a good actress?"

Her grandmother looked at her consideringly. "As to that, I think you *do* have talent. I've seen you in several plays and watched you work, here at home. The question you really want to ask, I think, is, 'Do I *want* to be an actress?' That is a question no one can answer but yourself, dearie." She paused thoughtfully before continuing. "I do think, though, that this summer *on your own* (were the words slightly stressed, or did Nan only imagine they were?) should give you an answer. As to the crowd—Betty and Daisy and Dan and Pete and all the others, they'll be here next year and not much changed. The change will be in you, if it is to be at all. So I'd say, welcome the chance, do your best and leave the rest to God."

"Thank you, Grandmother," Nan said sincerely. "You've made me feel better. I felt so uncertain, inside myself. It frightens me. Oh, of course I'm thrilled and it's an honor to be chosen, but I do feel that most of the students at the school are more sure than I am that they really want to go on the stage. That's why it seems odd to me that I was the one who was picked. There are others, I know, who would give anything for this chance. Perhaps I might even turn it down, except that I know how terribly it would disappoint Mother."

"Yes, it would. She's very happy about it."

"But, Grandmother, if after this summer's experience, I

should decide against the stage later on, how would Mother feel then?"

"Oh, she'd be disappointed, of course. But mothers learn to accept the growing up of their children. It is a large part of being a mother. I'll tell you something—" Grandmother hesitated, and Nan, sensing a real confidence, asked eagerly, "What, Grandmother?"

"Well, I had to learn to accept your father, Nan. I'd always thought your mother would marry a boy she knew and had grown up with; but nobody but Jim interested her, once she met him. So she married him and moved here, to New York, and when your grandfather died, I came here to live. You were just two then; your father died when you were four. Do you remember him at all, Nan?"

"Only a little bit, really. I remember his holding my hand at the zoo once—I think it was in the lion house and I was frightened, because that memory is filled with the smell of the lion house and a roar. I remember Father dragging me uphill on a sled once and I remember Mother crying when he died. That is all, really."

"Yes. Well, he was the very finest son-in-law I could have had and he made your mother very happy. I'm glad I was here to see that. He was a New Yorker, a business man, almost twenty years older than your mother, Nan. He was so assured, so 'set' in his ways. I felt there was no romance in the affair. I was wrong. So, if what you do makes you happy and is right for you, your mother will find it out, too. Just give yourself this chance, because she does so want it for you and she has been a good mother. It's not like marriage, dearie, not forever. Besides, you haven't any other very definite desire, have you?"

"No, not really, just to have fun, I guess."

Grandmother smiled. "Wouldn't surprise me a bit if you

found that the easiest thing to do, almost anywhere, at your age."

The ringing of the phone interrupted their talk, but Nan was to think of it often in the months that followed.

It was Betty on the phone and Nan told her the news.

"How marvelous! Oh, Nan, a real actress; with a real company! Do come over to my place and have lunch and I'll call the gang up and we'll make a party of it. Please, Nan?"

So it was arranged and Nan, bathing and dressing, began to recapture the satisfaction of the evening before. Now it seemed important that she was in this position—the first of the crowd to really step out into life, even if only for a summer.

She dressed carefully and unconsciously she became just a bit affected, just a bit the "actress" and this slight but subtle difference in her looks and manner set her apart from her close friends, so that it was a little as if she had already left them.

Nan enjoyed the luncheon party and yet seemed to be looking in at the whole afternoon. It was odd and a bit disconcerting, because no longer could her friends say, "Let's go here, or there, next week, Nan," or, "Shall we try to sail down to New London, this summer?" Instead, they could only say, "Do you remember when—" and "I suppose you'll meet lots of famous people," or "What's it really like to act?"

Already she was half a stranger!

Nan was actually relieved when the afternoon was over and Pete took her home. They didn't say much on the way and when they reached the lower hallway, Pete made a last plea.

"Nan, do you really want to go on with this crazy idea?"

Perhaps if he had phrased it differently she could at least have admitted her doubts to him. As it was, she only said evenly, "I'm sure, Pete."

There was a moment's awkward pause and then Nan asked, "You'll write me, won't you?"

"Oh, sure, I'll write, if you will—"

Both of them knew it was only a gesture, that the writing would not bring them closer together. Pete said good-by quickly and left. But as the elevator bore Nan upwards she knew she did not have any real pang in parting from him. Instead, she was eager only to know whether her mother was home yet.

As it happened, she had not returned from work, but there were two telephone messages for Nan. One was from Mark Byron, and the other from Alicia Van Delyss.

"Are you sure that was the name of the girl who called?" Nan asked her grandmother.

"It's not likely I'd think up a name like that all by myself, is it?" her grandmother replied.

"No, but—you did hear her name last night. She was the dark girl with the long hair who received a contract from the same company I'm to be in."

"I didn't pay much attention to the names, to tell you the truth, but I do remember her. She's the one who spoke to the audience, isn't she?"

"That's right."

"Struck me a bit bold."

"Oh, not bold!"

"We called it that in my day. I don't know what you call it now."

Nan giggled. "Maybe you're right. At any rate, I can't imagine what she wants with me."

"Going to the same company, aren't you? Doesn't seem so strange to me that she called you."

"But you don't know Alicia," Nan began and shrugged it off. "Oh, well, I'll call Mark first anyway."

Nan had always liked Mark and he was among the very few at the dramatic school that she had seen anything of outside of working hours.

Several times they had gone together to see a Broadway production (in the cheapest of balcony seats and strictly Dutch treat). They had lunched together quite often and once she had gone with him to his home to meet his family. It was a house full of youngsters, for Mark had six younger brothers and sisters.

Nan had loved his family instantly. The smiling, busy mother, the heavy-set, quiet father and all the children. They were such a contrast to her own family where she was the only child and there was no longer any father. It had surprised her to find out that Mark's real last name was not Byron, but a much longer Italian one. He had taken Byron for the stage. Later on, Nan was to discover that many of the people in the theater had such names, but, incredibly, Alicia's was her own!

As to Mark and Nan, there had been nothing the least bit sentimental about their friendship, so she was a little disturbed at herself to realize how glad she was that he had called and to remember that she had fallen asleep last night thinking of him. Now she went to the phone and dialed his number. As his voice answered, she could hear the sound of the children playing in the background.

"Mark? This is Nan Lane. You called when I was out."

"That's right. Nan, I've great news! I went downtown today and barged right into Mr. Murray's office. He's in town, you know—I found that out—and I've been signed on at the Murray Theater as assistant stage manager. Isn't that great?"

"Oh, Mark! How wonderful. Gee—it's, it's swell!"

"Are you really glad, Nan?"

"Of course I'm glad. I was dreading not knowing any-one there."

Some of the eagerness in his voice dimmed as he said, "Yes, yes, I suppose you would." Then a teasing note crept into it, "You know Alicia," he said.

"Oh, Mark! By the way, Alicia called me up too, while I was out. Whatever do you suppose she wants? I haven't called her back yet."

There was a silence on the other end of the phone and Nan asked, "Mark, are you there?"

"Yes, I'm here. Nan—I hate to be such a nasty cuss, but you do know Edith Trevor and Mr. Woolock."

"But I only met them—" Nan began, and then continued slowly, "Yes, yes, I see."

"Nan, I'm serious, that girl can be poison."

"I'm afraid you're right. What do I do?"

"Call her back and be pleasant, but don't tell her that you don't know, *really* know, those people. She'll not be-lieve you, or choose not to and you'll have made an enemy of her. Just don't be too cordial, that's all."

"Oh, Mark, I hate things like this! Are a lot of theater people like Alicia, do you suppose?"

"Only a few, still it's one of the reasons why I don't see you too clearly in the theater, in spite of your talent."

"You think I have talent?"

"Of course you have, but I'd hate to see you get even a little like Alicia and some others—hard and opportunistic."

"What about yourself? You're going into the theater."

"Yes, but I'm not really interested in the professional theater and not at all in acting."

"You're more interested in directing, aren't you?"

"Yes. And I've got ideas—great ideas, if they seem to be working out, I'll tell you about them—if you'd like to hear?"

"I'd love to, Mark."

"O.K. Anyway, I wanted to tell you I'd be in the same company for the summer. I'll try to see you this week if I can. I think I'll have to go out there before you, but that will mean I can be on hand to welcome you. I have to hang up now. My Ma is waiting supper for me."

"Bye, Mark."

"Bye."

Nan hung up the phone and stood quietly thinking. It would make all the difference in the world to have Mark in Metropolis. Not because he was a boy, she told herself firmly, but just because he was a good friend and nice— nice all the way through.

Might as well do it now and get it over with, Nan thought, and, smiling dreamily, she dialed Alicia's number. But Alicia was out.

5

Wardrobes and Advice

NAN HAD CHANGED HER CLOTHES and was helping to prepare dinner by the time her mother arrived home.

"Mother, the gang gave me a luncheon party today and Grandmother cooked me a late breakfast and Mark is going to the Murray Company, too!" Her news came out in an enthusiastic jumble. Her mother smiled. "I'm glad you had a good day, dear. You were sound asleep when I left. Nan, I've arranged to take three days off next week, to go shopping with you. I made some inquiries and I gather you will need to have a good wardrobe with you. Except for costume plays, you are expected to wear your own clothes. I spoke to Mr. Lloyd and the school will arrange to get you a room in Metropolis. There's a girls' residence club there, where some of the younger members stay."

"But, Mother, what about the money for all these clothes? Where will you get it?"

"Now don't you worry over that. That's my job. I can sell an extra article or so, I'm pretty sure. Anyway, what's a little money compared to your future?" Mother sounded so confident and gay that presently the more worrisome Nan fell into her mood.

Mother *was* pretty wonderful. It wasn't easy, Nan

knew, to support her, and grandmother too, yet mother always made it seem as if it were. Nan remembered how, when she was much younger, her mother had lost a job just before Christmas. Instead of moaning about it, she had gaily suggested making a game of it. Nan, her grandmother and she herself would buy all their presents that year from the five and ten. Object, to see who could get the best and most interesting presents for a dollar. Nan had thought it then—and remembered it now—as one of her most exciting Christmases. It was only later that she realized the "game" had been dictated by necessity.

The memory prompted her to go over and hug her mother before she asked, "What will we buy?"

Mrs. Lane ticked off the essentials on her fingers.

"A good suit. An afternoon dress. Several good hats. Two evening dresses. Sport clothes and some new every-day dresses. Shoes, accessories—"

"But, Mother—all those!"

"We'll see. What you already have needs augmenting, but some can be made to do, no doubt. Let's have supper first and then we'll clear out your closet and see what you already have there."

At supper, Nan told her mother about Mark and Alicia and herself and, to her relief, her mother agreed with Mark's judgment.

"In any business or profession there are always people like Alicia, Nan. As Mark says, they're poison, and because they are, you have to handle them carefully. Your Mark sounds as if he has a head on his shoulders."

"He's not *my* Mark," Nan protested, and flushed, but her mother did not seem to notice, and for this she was grateful.

The next week was such a maze of shopping that, excited as Nan had been about it at first, she was heartily glad when it was over.

She did love, though, the cobalt blue evening gown which brought out the highlights in her auburn hair and the more sophisticated black evening dress which her mother had considered essential. She spent happy hours showing off her new purchases to Betty and her other long-time friends, who were now frankly envious. Of Pete, she saw nothing.

Twice she phoned Alicia and twice Alicia was out. To her disappointment, Mark did not call again and she could not think of a good enough excuse to phone him.

At the end of the week, she and her mother went together to purchase the railway tickets. Pullman. It seemed wonderful to Nan, and quite unbelievable.

At last there were only four days left and to Nan it seemed they would never end.

On Sunday, grandmother cooked a gala meal and the three were very gay together.

Just before bedtime, mother came into Nan's room, carrying a large box. "This is something special and my gift to you," she said, handing it to Nan. "I would rather have given it to you when you left but it has to be packed in your trunk tomorrow."

Nan opened the package eagerly and found a beautiful make-up box. Leather covered, it had a mirror on the inside of the lid, which could be adjusted, high or low, and a full supply of make-up. Foundation cream, cleansing cream, make-up sticks of all shades, mascara, powder—all the very best brands.

Nan hugged her mother and came very close to crying. "Why, it's fit for a star!" she exclaimed, and added, "It's funny but one thing I like especially about the theater is the smell. Don't laugh, I mean it! The smell of grease paint and scenery; it's exciting, some way."

Her mother nodded in understanding.

"I wasn't going to laugh. As a newspaper woman, I know just what you mean. With us, it is the smell of hot oil on the presses and fresh newsprint and the smoke of many cigarettes. It's a special blend and the theater has its own."

"Mother, did you ever want to be an actress yourself?"

Mrs. Lane hesitated before replying. . . . "It's a little hard to say, Nan. I never really wanted to be anything but a wife to your father, but after he died, I did wish I'd had the training for the stage. I always loved it. You remember, I began to take you along with me to see good plays as soon as you were able to understand them at all? Your father and I had always enjoyed the theater together and he had exceptionally good judgment about it, so that he discussed both the plays and the acting with me. In the end, I grew to feel that I might well have developed along those lines myself; I even did a bit of Little Theater work before you were born. Then you came, and your father died while you were still so young, so I never pursued my bent."

"Would you have, if I hadn't been born? I mean, if you'd been a widow without a child?"

"What a terrible thought, Nan! I've no idea. All I know is that a friend of mine got me a chance in a newspaper office and gradually I've developed some competence there. I like it, too."

"I know you do, Mother, but I've sometimes wondered if I really have as much talent as you think, or whether you just hope I have. I mean, if it was something you wanted very much yourself?"

"I never wanted it that badly, Nan, honestly. Are you trying to tell me you do not want the theater, dear? Because I've never wanted to force anything on you."

Oddly enough, after having been as frank as this with her mother, Nan felt a great sense of relief.

"No, it's just that I'm not *sure*, Mother, that I can be as fine an actress as you hope. I was afraid that, because I showed talent, you thought I was absolutely *sure* I'd be a great actress and then if I wasn't, you'd be disappointed."

Mrs. Lane hugged her daughter and laughed. "Goodness, child! Of course you are not sure. You are very young yet. But you do have talent. You didn't want college, nor were you interested in a business course, so we chose this, or at least I thought *we* did. Anyway, you will be surer after this summer."

"I hope so, Mother. But I do feel better, now that I've told you my uncertainties."

"Good! Now, there's one more thing. I have a very dear friend who lives in Metropolis. I've not seen her in years. Margaret Stockton she is now, but I've written to her to say that you will be staying at the Shirley Arms. That is the name of the residence club for girls. It was built by a Mrs. Shirley for working girls. At any rate I've written Margaret that you are to be there and I've not had a chance to hear from her yet. She used to be lots of fun and I can't imagine her changing. She has a daughter about your age, or maybe a little younger, and, I believe, a lovely home. I'm going to write another letter to her for you to take along and it will serve to introduce you. Do look her up, for it will make me feel a great deal better to know that a grown-up whom I know will be seeing something of you from time to time. Also, in case of any illness, or other difficulty, which we pray won't happen, you could call on her. Well, sleep tight, dear. Tomorrow is the big day."

After her mother had left the room, Nan determined in her heart to do the very best she could during the summer ahead and, putting all doubts out of her mind, to take each day as it came.

U. S. 980024

6

The Train Trip and Alicia

JUST BEFORE THE TRAIN PULLED OUT the following day, her mother handed Nan an envelope containing the letter of introduction to her old friend, Margaret Stockton. Nan took the letter reluctantly, for she had no desire to use it. Now that she was about to go forth on her own, she wanted to be really independent.

However, as the miles clicked off under the train wheels Nan began to suffer the pangs of homesickness. One or two people, mostly elderly, spoke to her pleasantly, but Nan did not encourage them. She read until her eyes were tired and watched an uninteresting landscape unfold until it made her head nod in weariness.

It was a relief when she heard the first call to lunch.

Walking, swayingly, to the lavatory, Nan tidied up, fought a brief impulse to tears, then made her way to the diner.

She had scarcely glanced at the menu handed to her by the waiter, when a throaty voice said, "Nan Lane! I didn't know you were on this train." Before she turned, Nan knew it was Alicia—an Alicia turned out in a smart black suit, with a coral blouse and huge loop earrings to match.

Several of the diners had already glanced up and were frankly staring at the girl.

"Why, Alicia," Nan replied, "I didn't see you get on! Do sit down here."

"Oh, I got on at Philadelphia," Alicia explained, taking the seat opposite Nan. They were alone at the table. "I visited my father for a few days before starting out. My mother and father are divorced, you know."

Nan hadn't known and she was at a loss as to what to say. Did one respond with, "I'm sorry," or what? But she need not have worried for Alicia had gone on talking and, though she had missed several words, Nan caught the drift.

"—so of course *he* got me a compartment." Alicia laughed. It was a real laugh, though there was nothing of humor in what she said nor in her manner of saying it. "My parents are so stupid! It's so easy to play them off, one against the other, and they never even know I'm doing it! Father gave me a hunk of cash, too. Oh, I made out fine!" She picked up the menu and glanced at it. "Awful stuff they serve you on trains. I could have had lunch in my compartment but I thought it might be more fun to eat here. Do you have a roomette?"

"Goodness no!" Nan was startled into frankness. "I could never afford it."

"Well, you come into mine after lunch and we'll talk. It was a break for you, winning the scholarship, wasn't it?"

Nan nodded, not sure whether the remark was complimentary or not.

The waiter came along just then and they ordered. Suddenly Alicia asked, "Did you notice that man across the aisle, two tables down, staring at me?"

"Yes, I did."

"Looks as if he has money. Might be interesting to talk

to him. Suppose we go back to the observation car after lunch?"

"I thought you said—" Nan began.

"I know I did, my pet. But never waste your time on a girl when there's a man around. That's my motto and you might as well know it now."

That at least was frank. But what Alicia could see in a man so much older, apparently, than she was, Nan could not imagine. Nan sneaked a look at him. He was inclined toward stoutness and his hair was definitely receding.

With a sudden switch of thought (characteristic of all Alicia's conversations, Nan was to discover) Alicia now asked, "Where are you planning to stay in Metropolis?"

"I'm planning to stay at the Shirley Arms," Nan answered.

"The Shirley Arms? Oh, my pet, not the Shirley Arms! You might as well be in boarding school—ever been in a boarding school?"

Nan answered in the negative, and did not reveal that not so many years ago she had read countless stories about boarding school and, at the time, had passionately wished she were one of the fortunate girls sent to such a school.

"Well, I have and so I know whereof I speak, my pet. Horrible stuffy rules and stuffier girls. Not for me! I'm going to a hotel."

"Mother has a friend in Metropolis and I may spend some time with her," Nan offered in an unexpected flare of defensiveness.

But Alicia was not impressed.

"Really? Well, that's nice, I'm sure. Still, I'd rather be on my own. But then you're pretty young, aren't you?" But before Nan could answer the subject was abruptly switched again, and the question came which Nan had been dreading.

"Do tell me, how long have you known Miss Trevor? I saw her speaking to you the night of the graduation."

Cautiously Nan answered, "I've not known her very long. Mr. Woolock, however, is a very old friend of my mother's."

Alicia nodded, apparently pleased with some inner thought of her own, before she said, "I think you and I should see something of each other while we are out here with the company. Of course, I realize that I will be thrown more with the regular members of the company than you will, but with your backing, you are quite likely to receive some really good parts yourself. Yes, we really must keep in touch."

Nan opened her mouth to make an angry reply, then closed it again as she remembered Mark's advice—and her mother's. At present, Alicia would never believe that she did not have influence. Only time would show her that. Meanwhile, Nan herself had nothing either to lose or gain by keeping silence. She was spared the necessity of making even a conventional reply by the waiter depositing their food in front of them.

Conversation died as the two ate their meal in silence. Nan was amused to note that Alicia seemed quite as hungry as she was herself and ate the "awful stuff" with a good appetite. Nan couldn't help wondering if it were not that way with Alicia in many matters. Perhaps she felt compelled, for some reason, to appear always the scoffer, while underneath she was no more sure of herself than any other person. The thought rather comforted Nan and made her disposed to feel more kindly toward her companion until, as they were finishing their meal, the man down the aisle rose and, just as he came opposite them, Alicia's purse slid off her lap so that he nearly stepped on it. He stooped over and, picking it up, held it out to Alicia, smiling.

"So awkward of me! Thank you," Alicia said, as she accepted it from his hands.

"Not at all awkward," the man replied, which seemed to Nan an odd remark.

"I see you two young ladies have nearly finished your meal," he continued. "Wouldn't you like to walk back to the observation car for a bit? I'm a rather lonesome chap just now and I'd welcome such lovely company."

"I'd like to very much. Train trips are such a bore—unless, of course, one meets someone interesting," Alicia answered.

"My name is Harry Torley, and I can't guarantee how interesting I'll be—but I can try."

"I am Alicia Van Delyss, and this is Nan Lane," Alicia said, then added, "We are on our way to Metropolis to join the Murray Stock Company, where I am to act and Miss Lane is a student."

"Now that's wonderful! If you've never been out there before, I can really show you the town. I live there and I've attended the shows at the Murray every year."

Alicia had by now finished her coffee and she rose.

"Won't you join us, Miss Lane?" Mr. Torley asked.

Nan had assumed from the beginning that she and Alicia would stay together, but now she was subtly made to feel she was an extra.

"Why, thank you, no—I—I have some letters to write and—and—" She stammered in her embarrassment. Actually, she was shocked that Alicia should be willing to go off with a strange man. It was something she had been warned about since her childhood. It was something no sensible girl ever did and certainly she did not intend to join Alicia in any such affair.

"See you at the theater, my pet," Alicia said, in evident relief and, turning her head as she followed the man down the aisle, she winked, actually winked, at the still astounded Nan.

Well, Nan thought, as she made her way back to her own seat, at least that encounter cured me of homesickness!

For a while Nan was absorbed in alternately watching the scenery and covertly observing the passengers in the other seats. Although she had rebuffed those few who had spoken to her, it was mostly because she was timid, on this her first long trip alone. Now she watched them and tried to figure out what they were like—even to imagine a life for them. As darkness fell, however, Nan got down her suitcase from the overhead rack and, taking out the writing case her mother had provided, she did in fact write home and, in addition, sent several cards to her friends.

In the diner that night, Nan saw no sign of Alicia and, striking up a conversation with a nice older woman at her table, she went back to sit with her a bit. It was only a little past ten, though, when Nan asked the porter to make up her berth and she gratefully stretched out on it. The journey was tiring, she discovered, and she would be glad to be at her destination in the morning.

Nan had received clear instructions as to how to reach the Shirley Arms and she went directly there upon her arrival in Metropolis, having seen no further sign of Alicia. She was considerably surprised when she reached the residence club to receive a message from Mrs. Stockton, asking her to phone as soon as she came in. Evidently, Mrs. Stockton had received Mother's letter and was not waiting for Nan to contact her.

Nan was shown into a small, plain, but not uncomfortable room, which overlooked a small park. It had a basin with running water, and the bathroom was just down the hall.

"I'm sure you'll like it here, Miss Lane," the house mother said. "We have some lovely girls staying with us. Right now, we have no one registered from the Murray but we have had. There's a cafeteria on the ground floor and parlors and a nice library of books, so just feel free to use them. I'll introduce you to some of the girls later on. It's early now and they're mostly business girls, so they are not in yet."

"Thank you. That's awfully nice of you. I'm sure I'll like it here," Nan said—and meant it. "And could you tell me where the phone is so that I can answer this message I received from a friend of my mother's?"

"Right down the hall and turn to your right, dear. Now, I'll leave you to settle in. See you later."

"Thank you," Nan said again. As soon as the door was closed she went over and sat on the bed with its crisp white spread. It was all so strange to her. A room with no one she knew nearby; in a house full of strange girls and yet—it *was* fun in a way. Nan got up and walked to the window, where she stood looking down on the people on the street below and in the park across the street. It looked much to her as sections of New York looked, or Brooklyn, maybe— city-like private houses, with no grounds, some two, some four stories high, a cement-paved park with benches occupied now by what looked like the same mothers and children and elderly men and women who sat on such benches in New York.

After a bit, Nan turned from the window, opened her bag, took out her bureau things and arranged them on the walnut dresser. She hung up her hat and coat and then hesitated.

Out loud she said, "What I need is a good hot bath," and was startled at her own voice in the silence. Grinning to herself, she began to collect her bath things. From down the hall came the sound of a girl's laughter and a voice said, " 'Bye, be seeing you." Then there was the slam of a door.

Maybe I'd better make that call to Mrs. Stockton first Nan thought, and, picking up the paper with the message on it, she left her room and made her way to the telephone.

7

A New Home

LESS THAN AN HOUR after Nan had picked up the telephone in the Shirley Arms and called Mrs. Stockton's number, she found herself seated beside that lady in her car, being driven rapidly and expertly through the traffic of downtown Metropolis.

"—and so you see, it couldn't be better," Mrs. Stockton was saying. "Here I was, missing Sue—and yet I know she'll just *love* camp, I did at her age; though at first I thought I should hate it! I can't think what possessed Laura not to send you directly to me. Not that the Shirley Arms isn't a perfectly *respectable* place—but surely no place to meet people—and at your age one does so want to meet people, don't you think?"

Nan opened her mouth to reply and closed it again as Mrs. Stockton continued to talk steadily.

"It's just two blocks farther to your new home."

Nan looked with interest at the houses on either side of the street. They were, for the most part, set well back in spacious grounds. Each house seemed to be vying with the other in the matter of gardens, all of which were a riot of lovely blooms. There was no doubt that this section of

44

town was a most choice one. Even a total stranger could tell that.

Mrs. Stockton braked for a traffic light as she said, "Jim will be so thrilled to have you—just as thrilled as I am. He misses Sue ever so much. I'm sorry we can't break our dinner date for tonight, on such short notice, but Annie will get you a meal, and you'll likely need to rest anyway after the trip."

The light changed and the car eased into motion again, traveled half a block and swerved into the driveway of a charming, low field-stone house. Mrs. Stockton had opened the door almost before Nan realized that they had arrived.

"Here we are! Now, just leave your bag there. Harry will bring it in and he'll pick up your trunk at the Shirley Arms tomorrow," Mrs. Stockton said.

Bewildered and completely overwhelmed, Nan followed her mother's friend into the house. The room they entered from the hall was one of the loveliest she had ever seen. Furnished with deep divans and chairs upholstered in a soft delft-blue, the many-hued oriental rug and gold curtains, gave it warmth. There were oil paintings on the walls. A single glance told Nan that they were truly good. At one side of the room, there was a wide fireplace, banked with flowers.

"Jim, Jim," Mrs. Stockton called, as she took off her gloves and rang for the maid.

Nan stood uncertainly just inside the doorway as Mr. Stockton came in another door and the maid in still another.

"Jim, this is Laura's child—Laura Lane. Her name is Nan and she is going to stay with us. You remember I read you Laura's letter? Nan, this is my husband, Jim."

Mr. Stockton came forward with outstretched hand. He was a tall, graying man, who looked very big beside his small wife, as she stood on tiptoe to kiss him, before he shook Nan's hand.

"Glad to have you here, my dear," he said, with every appearance of cordiality, as if suddenly acquiring a house guest was an everyday event.

"Annie, will you just see that Miss Sue's room is ready? And you might fix us some tea," Mrs. Stockton rattled on. "Miss Nan's bag is in the car. You'll tell Harry? And, Annie, Miss Nan will have to eat alone tonight—I'm sorry but it can't be helped this time. Now, child, do let's sit down and get acquainted, and you must tell me *all* about yourself."

Mrs. Stockton led Nan to the inviting divan, patting the seat beside her, so Nan sat down. Mr. Stockton sat in a wing chair nearby, and, to her surprise, Nan found presently that Mrs. Stockton was not only a great talker but a good listener as well. Over tea, Nan told her hosts all about her trip and even made an amusing tale of her encounter with Alicia.

Mrs. Stockton chuckled delightedly. "Your Alicia will probably be a little more attentive to you now—wouldn't you think, Jim?" she asked, which remark, for the moment went completely over Nan's head, though she was to remember it later.

Mrs. Stockton questioned Nan skillfully about her mother, about her own ambitions and life, and she was so obviously interested and warmhearted that her guest's initial shock of resentment at being so suddenly taken charge of completely evaporated in gratitude for such interest.

Mrs. Stockton showed Nan her daughter's picture. Sue was a few years younger than Nan and looked like a very pleasant girl.

After the tea things were cleared away, Mrs. Stockton herself took Nan to her room. It was certainly a contrast to the room at the Shirley Arms she had so recently left, Nan thought. It was the sort of room every girl dreams of. From the pineapple four-poster bed to the ruffled dressing table and gay patterned curtains at the casement windows. It was perfect, so perfect that Nan ventured a heartfelt protest.

"But, Mrs. Stockton, will Sue like me to take her room?"

"My dear child, she'd be delighted. I thought you'd like her room so much better than any of the guest rooms. It's made for a young girl and, besides, we never know when we'll have guests staying a night or so. Much better for you to be here and Sue wouldn't mind a bit, I assure you. She's easygoing, not a possessive bone in her body."

To herself Nan thought that this was a good thing, with a mother who blithely turned over her daughter's room to a complete stranger!

"Now I'll just leave you. The bath is right down the hall and there are plenty of magazines in the living room, besides Sue's books right over there—if they are not too young for you. Tomorrow we'll talk about when you have to go to work and all that. I suppose you'll go to Mass?"

Nan answered she would.

"All right—you tell Annie what time you want to be wakened. Harry can drive you. We sleep late and go to eleven o'clock service ourselves. Now just relax and Annie will call you when dinner is ready. Oh, do you know anyone in Metropolis—beside your precious Alicia, I mean?"

Nan told her about Mark.

"*Mmmm.* I suppose you'll see him on Monday. Oh, I know lots of young people for you to meet. It's going to be so much fun having you here! Now, I'd better run, or I'll never be ready in time, and Jim just hates to be kept waiting. Now, if you need anything at all, just call Annie—see, the bell pull is right here by the door, and Annie will be in all night. 'Bye, now. See you tomorrow."

Slowly Nan walked over and sat down in the chair beside the desk. On a rack at the foot of her bed lay her suitcase, so there was no mistake, she was really here, in the Stockton home! I wonder, Nan thought, just how long I'll feel like Cinderella, or if, like her, I'll suddenly wake and find myself by the ashes—or rather back in the Shirley Arms!

It was hard to sort out the impressions of the past few hours. They had been like a kaleidoscope; one piece rapidly following another to make new patterns.

Mrs. Stockton was obviously "an arranger and runner" of things, if what had passed was any indication.

She was a tiny blonde woman, beautifully groomed, who moved fast, talked fast, drove fast and yet radiated a real warmth. Nan could not help but like her; yet, at the same time, she could not help wondering just how much of her life Mrs. Stockton would now undertake to run for her. Mr. Stockton was so quiet by comparison with his wife that Nan did not have a really clear impression of him, aside from his obvious good looks.

Prompted by curiosity, Nan rose and looked at a group of framed photographs hung near the dressing table. They were all of the family. Some showed Sue much younger and some must have been taken recently, but in all of them she looked relaxed and happy.

"Well, Sue, I hope you *really* don't mind my being here, for it surely is an adventure," Nan said softly, before she began to unpack and hang up her clothes, for the second time that day.

Down the hall, Nan had a luxurious bath, slipped into a simple dress and was quite prepared for dinner when Annie came to the door to announce it.

It was the first time in her life that Nan had sat down alone for dinner in a private house and been served—served, moreover, a complete meal, from soup to dessert.

She longed to talk to Annie, who looked kind, but being too shy to do so, ate in silence. . . . She was heartily glad when the meal was over, even though the evening still loomed ahead of her.

It wasn't until the dessert was being cleared away that Annie said, "There's a radio in the living room, if you'd care for it, Miss. Or, if it's readin' you want, there's plenty of that."

"Thank you—I—I guess I'll write home and then read a bit. And, Annie, Mrs. Stockton said you'd wake me in time for church and the chauffeur would drive me there; but I have no idea where my church is, or whether I could go there myself."

That broke the ice, as it developed that Annie went to the same church. She agreed to walk there with Nan, who much preferred this arrangement to being driven by the chauffeur.

"Mrs. Stockton is the kindest hearted lady you could find, anywhere at all," Annie declared. "I've worked for them long years now an' I couldn't say how many the Missus has befriended. Don't you worry a bit about takin' Miss Sue's room, or about their entertainin' you. If it wasn't you, it'd be someone else. Sure, they've plenty of money an' time, an' it's a pleasure to them. Not all rich folks are like that—I've worked for them that would grudge you a crust—but not here. But look, Miss Nan—you don't mind if I tell you somethin'?"

"I'd be glad, Annie. You see, this was all so sudden. I never even met Mrs. Stockton before, and here I am in her house—"

"It's this. From what you say, you have to go to work at that theater? Don't let the Missus be takin' you from it; if you get my meanin'? She never had to work; but maybe you'll have to?"

"Yes, yes, I will, Annie. My mother is a widow and she works and I'll have to work, too, as soon as I'm old enough and have finished my training."

Annie nodded in sympathy and understanding.

"Well then, you just be firm about what you have to do. She'll like you the better for it—an'—an' don't be takin' her matchmakin' too serious either; she's a great one for that, the Missus is!"

Nan laughed delightedly, "Oh, Annie—I'm too young for that," she said.

"Indeed an' you're not—pretty as you are—but you don't look like your head would be turned easy."

"I hope not," Nan answered soberly, then added, "Thank you, Annie, and I do hope I don't make too much extra trouble for you."

"That you won't indeed. I miss Sue an' her young friends. Well, I'll be clearin' up now, but I'm close by. If you need me, just ring."

So Nan spent a snug evening, reading and writing home, before she went to bed.

8

The Club

NAN AND ANNIE had gone to church and returned. As Nan lay in a deck chair outside on the patio, after a hearty breakfast, she thought how like home the place already seemed to her—perhaps because she had been to church, and also because she was a part of a family. And in Annie she felt she had found a friend. She could not help wondering whether she would have felt at home so quickly at the residence club. It was near twelve-thirty when Mrs. Stockton returned from church and came directly to the patio.

"Good morning, Nan dear. Did you sleep well?"

"I certainly did, thank you."

"And you've been up for ages, I suppose? After brunch Jim and I will drive you out to the club and around town a bit."

"Oh, please don't go to any trouble for me—really I'm very happy right here."

"Nonsense! Glad to show you our town. We're rather proud of it, even though it isn't as big as New York—and we generally spend the afternoon at the club. Jim likes his golf. Do you play?"

"No, I don't."

"Tennis?"

"Yes, I love it."

"Good! We've extra rackets any time you care to use them. I hope you brought a bathing suit?"

"Yes, I did; though Mother wasn't sure that this far inland there would be a place to swim."

"We've quite a nice outdoor pool at the club. You will be our guest, so that's settled. Now is there anything you want?"

"No, indeed— Oh, yes, there's one thing. I would like to get my bearings so that I can reach the theater tomorrow. The first rehearsal is called for ten o'clock. Is there a bus I can take from here?"

A minute frown appeared on Mrs. Stockton's face and then quickly cleared.

"Ten? Oh, then Harry can drive you. He'll have time to get back here after he takes Jim to the office."

Remembering Annie's advice, Nan made her voice as firm as possible. "But Mrs. Stockton, I'd rather go by bus—if I can. I will have to get there every day, you know."

"The first day then, Harry will show you the way. Now let me see, what will you do for lunch tomorrow?"

Nan suppressed a desire to giggle.

"Oh, don't worry over that, Mrs. Stockton. I'll eat whatever the rest do."

Mrs. Stockton looked at Nan with somewhat the same expression with which a mother cat looks at a kitten. "You're much too thin," she pronounced, "and I doubt if you will eat properly—I know young people—but we will see to it that you eat a good breakfast and a decent dinner, at any rate. Now, just relax and I'll call you when we are ready to go."

Nan was still in the deck chair and half asleep when Annie came out with some sandwiches, fruit and milk for her lunch. After she had eaten them, Mrs. Stockton called her inside.

"Have you any sports dresses with you, dear?" she asked.

Nan was glad to be able to answer "yes" to that and went to put on one of the new dresses she and her mother had bought. It was a white sharkskin, with a touch of green on the collar, belt and pocket. Mrs. Stockton liked it and said so.

After Nan dressed, she and Mrs. Stockton got into the car, with Mr. Stockton driving this time. Nan was shown downtown Metropolis and driven past the Murray Theater, an imposing structure of Moorish architecture and so large that a sinking feeling came into her stomach as she thought of how many people it would hold.

Then they drove out to the club, which proved to be a luxurious country club. Mrs. Stockton introduced Nan to everyone they met on the path to the clubhouse and finally her confused young guest gave up trying to remember names. It was only after Mr. Stockton had gone out onto the links and she and Mrs. Stockton were seated on the wide veranda that Nan began to relax.

"So, you are an actress at the Murray. How exciting!" a pleasant, spectacled girl sitting next to Nan said.

"Not exactly," Nan demurred, "I'm a sort of student there."

"I didn't know Mr. Murray ran a *school* now," a cool voice commented, then added with a knowing laugh, "Not but what some of the shows he puts on aren't amateurish enough!"

Nan flushed and declared firmly, "I've never seen any of

his productions, but in New York his reputation is excellent, and his stars are considered among the best to be had. He always has a certain number of students, I believe, and I'm very glad to be one of them this year."

"My what an honor that must be!" the owner of the cool voice said, and Nan saw that she was a very pretty, but discontented looking girl of about her own age.

"Stow it, Sal," one of the young men in the group broke in. "Your envy is showing."

Suddenly the girl's face changed entirely, "I'm sorry," she said impulsively to Nan. "Jud is right. I *am* envious. I wanted to attend a dramatic school the worst way and, instead, Mother sent me to a *foul* boarding school. Maybe you could tell me a bit about the theater? Did you attend dramatic school?"

"I do," Nan answered, instantly forgiving the pretty blonde, "in New York. Maybe when I know my way around you could come backstage with me?"

"Oh, I'd love it! Look, my name is Sally Holly—that's easy to remember, isn't it? I tell you the theater is all I dream about, day and night—and you wait, I'll get there yet!"

There was so much sincerity and force to Sally that Nan could well believe she meant it. Once more she felt humble, that she, who was not so dedicated, should have the opportunity others longed for.

It was apparent that Sally would have monopolized Nan, then and there, except that inside band music began to play on the phonograph.

"Come on, let's dance," the boy called Jud suggested and in a moment Nan had a partner and so the afternoon passed very pleasantly indeed.

At dinner that evening, Nan had a chance to ask Mrs. Stockton about the various young people she had met, and especially about Sally Holly.

"Sally is dear," Mrs. Stockton said, "and I only hope her mother will come to her senses about her. You see, her mother was an actress herself, many years ago. She married a man with a great deal of money and now she doesn't want Sally to have anything to do with the theater. She wants something quite different for her. But ever since Sally was able to walk and talk, she has acted. I think her mother would like to see her married to Jud Tompkins, but Sally won't be happy if she does that. Jud's all right, and he has money, but he's really very lazy and, for all Sally's good looks, she's serious minded. She's getting bitter and caustic, all because she can't have what she wants, can't even try to prove that she has talent. Perhaps you could be friendly with her. Not everyone likes her."

"I did. Not at first, but later. Only will Mrs. Holly like my being friendly with her?"

Mrs. Stockton laughed, and there was an edge to her voice as she answered, "Oh, Marlene Holly will be glad to have Sally go around with a friend of mine. Marlene is a climber—rather like your Alicia, my dear."

They left it at that and after thanking both the Stocktons for her wonderful afternoon, Nan went to bed early, to be ready for her big tomorrow.

Before she fell asleep she lay quietly, going over the day just past in her mind and trying to sort out her impressions. It was obvious that the Stocktons were "somebody" in this town. They had, Nan suspected, more than just money, they had "position." She determined to write to her mother and ask for fuller information about them.

As to the people she had met at the club, she liked Sally

and the solemn girl in glasses who had sat next to her on the veranda—Mary Riner was her name. One or two of the young men were pleasant, but by and large they seemed to her not nearly so nice as the students at the Booth—or even her young friends at home. It wasn't fair to judge on such short acquaintance, she knew. Anyway, she thought sleepily, I'll see Mark tomorrow—and won't Alicia be surprised if she sees me driving up with a chauffeur! On which engaging thought she fell asleep.

9

First Day

NAN WAS QUITE UNABLE to eat the substantial breakfast Annie set before her the next morning.

"You feel all right, Miss Nan? You haven't hardly eaten anything and Mrs. Stockton left word you were to have a good breakfast," Annie said.

"I'm sorry, Annie. I just can't eat. I'm too excited, I suppose—and it's a lovely breakfast, too. I *am* sorry."

"Well, so long as you feel good. I know the first time I went out in service I had terrible butterflies in my stomach, I was so afraid I'd do somethin' wrong. I'll offer up a prayer for you."

"Please do, Annie." Nan smiled gratefully, "You *do* understand."

"Indeed and I do. Now you just get ready and Harry'll be back in plenty of time."

Nan left her half-eaten breakfast and went to her room. Once there, she argued with herself. "How silly can you get? You are not doing a thing but report at the theater. If you grow this nervous now, whatever will you do when you do get a part?" Argument with herself did no good, however, so Nan began to dress. She was ready long before Harry put in an appearance. She wished now that she

had insisted on going by herself; it would have occupied
the time. Then what Annie had said came back to her and
she knew what she had to do.

Quietly, she knelt at the foot of her bed and prayed—
prayed that this summer she would be able to do her best;
prayed that she would find an answer for the question that
so beset her. *Is acting right for me? Is it what I really
want? Am I really good enough?*

So absorbed was she that Annie had to knock twice to
tell her that Harry and the car were waiting. Nan left
then, feeling calmer.

She was so occupied with her thoughts, however, that
she forgot to note the streets as they drove through them,
until Harry drew the car to a stop at the side entrance to
the Murray. He got out and held the door open for Nan.
As she stepped out of the car her first upward glance fell
upon Mark, walking toward her.

Never had she been so glad to see anyone!

"Mark!" she breathed and clung to his outstretched hand.

"I called the Shirley Arms and they said you'd left," he
exclaimed. "Whatever happened to you? I've been standing outside here for the past hour. I almost called the po-
lice! What happened?" And Mark bent a baleful glance
on Harry.

"Oh, Mark—wait till I tell you! You'll never believe it.
And I've been so scared—"

"Scared!" Mark took a step forward. "Who scared
you?"

"Oh, Mark, nobody scared me! I was scared of *today*—
of the theater! Stage fright, silly. Mark, this is Harry and
he's the chauffeur for my friends and he very kindly drove
me here today."

Mark relaxed, but he still looked dazed. Nan turned to

Harry. "You know," she said, "I have absolutely *no* idea of how we got here, so how will I ever get back?"

Harry smiled broadly. "If you'll tell me when you're to be through, Miss, I could call for you."

"Oh, good heavens, no! I mean, thank you, but I don't know when I'll get through and I've got to learn my way home."

"Very well, Miss. Now," Harry pointed, "down there two blocks you get the bus for—"

Mark interrupted. "You'd better tell me," he suggested, "and I'll guarantee to bring her home this afternoon. I don't think she's capable of taking in directions right now, do you?"

Harry grinned. "Guess you're right," he agreed and gave his directions to Mark, for which Nan was grateful.

The two men were still talking together, with Nan standing beside them, when Alicia stepped out of a cab. She saw Nan and Mark and the chauffeur, but, to Nan's amazement, gave her only the briefest of nods and went on into the theater.

Nan was still staring after her as Harry drove off and Mark took her elbow.

"Now, young lady, suppose you let me in on the secret of your sudden disappearance—to say nothing of your sudden wealth!"

"Mark," Nan said, ignoring his questions for the moment, "whatever do you suppose is the matter with Alicia? I was on the train on the way out with her, and she was very friendly. Of course, she ditched me for a man, but then she's Alicia. To tell you the truth, I was sort of hoping she'd be impressed with me rolling up in a chauffeur-driven car. She upstaged me so dreadfully when I told her I would be at the Shirley Arms."

"I don't think that Alicia includes chauffeurs among her friends," Mark remarked drily.

"But he *isn't* my friend—" catching a glimpse of the expression on Mark's face, Nan started all over again. "I don't mean he couldn't be, Mark, I mean he's the Stocktons' chauffeur. He just drove me here today so I couldn't help thinking I'd like to upstage Alicia for a change."

"And just who are the Stocktons?" Mark asked, a trifle grimly.

"Oh, Mark, of course, you don't even know! Look, are we late?"

"No, early, as a matter of fact. Let's have a cup of coffee at that soda fountain over there in the drugstore. Then you can try to enlighten me. O.K.?"

With a steaming cup of coffee and a muffin in front of her, Nan told her story.

"So," Mark said, when she had finished, "you've landed in a really soft spot, Nan. I'm glad for you."

He didn't sound too pleased, though, and Nan was frankly puzzled. It was a soft spot, true, but it had not been her own doing and the Stocktons were ever so nice and generous. Nan had not thought Mark mean-spirited, and now his attitude made her uncomfortable.

"Have you been inside the theater?" she asked, to change the subject.

Mark came alive then and eagerly described the backstage area.

"I suppose," he wound up, "it's not so modern, according to Broadway standards, but beside our little stage at the school, it's wonderful! And the stage manager is a grand guy. I think I'll get on well with him. Come on, finish your coffee. We'd better be going in."

On the way across the street Nan asked, "Where are you staying, Mark?"

"At a boarding house, of course. It's the only place in a town of this size that fits my pocketbook and is decent. I like it!" Again, Nan noticed he sounded belligerent.

The first person Nan actually met in the theater was "Mr. Mac," the stage doorman. He was sitting on a sturdy kitchen chair, propped at a dangerous angle against the side wall of the little entryway. Tipped rakishly on one side of his head was a bowler hat of the derby type, which Nan had never actually seen worn before.

"Mr. Mac," Mark said, holding Nan's arm in a firm grip, "this is Nan Lane. She is a student here for the summer and an old friend of mine. Nan, this is Mr. Mac."

Mr. Mac lowered his chair with a bang, rose and removed his hat, revealing an almost completely bald head. Bowing low to the astonished Nan, who had no idea who he was, he said, "I'm happy to make your acquaintance, Nan Lane. You'll find old Mac never forgets a face or a name. The passing parade passes me each year and they all know old Mac. The great, and the failures. I know them all. Your face is your pass to this the-ay-ter now, Miss, and may God give you good luck in it." Having made this speech, he replaced his hat, tipped back once more in his chair and asked in a normal voice, "This your first time in the the-ay-ter, Miss?"

"Yes, it is," Nan answered, "that is, the real theater."

"Well, young Mark here is a good one to show you about. I'd do it myself, except it's my duty to be right here." He pulled a large, old-fashioned watch from the vest he wore over his shirt. "Fifteen minutes, you've got still," he said.

Nan murmured her pleasure at having met him and followed Mark. The small hallway they had entered led into a square vestibule. From the farther end of this vestibule, iron, fire-escape type stairs ascended. On either side of these stairs there was a closed door, each with a star painted on it.

Mark began his explanations.

"Those two doors are the dressing rooms for the stars— the leading man and the leading woman. Only the ingenue, the juvenile lead and the character man have dressing rooms of their own, besides the stars. The other rooms hold two or more people. You'll probably find yourself all the way at the top! Now, over here is an important spot." Mark led Nan to a bulletin board. On it, beside the rather dog-eared and fly-specked Fire Department Regulations, were tacked a number of fresh notices. One was the notice of today's "first reading and casting" of *The Girl of the Golden West*.

"It's up to all of us to look at this bulletin board on entering and leaving the theater," Mark told Nan. "On it are put all notices of changes in rehearsal time, etc. Also, things like lost and found notices and anything else of importance."

"I'll be sure to look every time," Nan promised.

"Now, the stage is through here." Mark held open a door next to the bulletin board and Nan passed through to see for the first time a real stage from the back. It was impressive, to say the least—a bare stretch of board floor, a yawning gap where the curtain would be and beyond that the shadowy rows of seats. Nan walked to the edge of the apron and looked up. Above her, by the light of the single, unshaded electric bulb, on a stand in the center of the stage, she could see that there were two balconies in the theater.

"Oh, Mark—it's huge!" she breathed, awed.

Mark laughed. "It is, somewhat," he agreed. "But don't

forget that, with the footlights on, you'll be able to see only the first few rows of seats, and those not too clearly." He took her elbow and turned her around so that her back was to the darkened theater. On each side were two curtains, falling straight down, with a space between them. At the back there was a part of a cottage scene, still set up, and to one side a stack of "flats," huge, screenlike affairs, with their backs numbered and indicated; #5—Bar * Girl of the Golden West—Nan read on the one now uppermost.

"Those babies are a part of my job," Mark told her proudly. "See the set for the 'Girl,' well, by tomorrow or the next day, those will be set up here. Do you know who's playing the lead?"

Nan shook her head.

"Una Fair," Mark said, and Nan was suitably impressed.

At that moment there was a burst of laughter from the darkness out in front. It startled Nan. "Mark, are they laughing at us?" she asked anxiously.

Mark grinned. "No, that's from the rehearsal room and we had better get along." Nan followed him across the stage in the opposite direction from the one from which they had entered. They passed between the long curtains on that side and were in an area almost as large as the stage itself. Against the walls of this area, the wings as it was called, more flats were stacked, and also properties, such as chairs and tables.

"Watch your step now," Mark warned. "It's dim here and the stairs are steep."

It was indeed dim and Nan was glad to hold Mark's hand as he led her down a short flight of stairs, lighted only by a red sign saying EXIT. Beyond this, they passed in back of the box seats and then up the side aisle to the front of the theater. Here they descended another flight of stairs and, opening a door and holding it for Nan to pass through, Mark ushered her into the greenroom, as custom dictated this rehearsal room be called.

It was full of chattering groups of men and women, but before Nan could begin to search out any familiar face Mark led her to a window sill, on which a boy and a girl already sat.

"Shove over," Mark ordered good-naturedly, "this is Nan Lane—same school as mine. Nan, Bud Parks and Helen Graves. Be seeing you, Nan."

To Nan's dismay, Mark left the three of them, to join an older man standing at one side of the room. Nan rightly guessed that he was the stage manager. She half-jumped and was half-pulled onto the wide window ledge, between the two young people Mark had introduced to her.

10

Mark's Odd Behavior

THE NEXT HALF-HOUR was bewildering to Nan. With Mark no longer at her side, she felt lost.

Mr. Murray, the director, gave a brief welcome to the assembled company. He seemed nervous and in a hurry. Nan could, of course, identify Una Fair, who sat almost directly opposite her, on a divan. Next to her was the leading man, Hartley Bennett. Nan thought that the girl sitting on a chair close to Miss Fair must be Peggy Worth, just beginning to be known for her ingenue roles. She looked older than Nan had expected, however.

Having given his brief welcome, Mr. Murray called Joe Maguire, his stage manager and Mark's direct "boss," to him.

"Check attendance," he ordered briefly and immediately busied himself with some papers spread on the desk before him.

Mr. Maguire held a sheet of paper in his hand and from it he called off the names of the company. He started with the principals and Nan found that she had been right in her guess as to Peggy Worth. She listened carefully and tried to catch each "here" or "present" and identify the person who had spoken. She was so absorbed in the effort that she

65

almost missed answering when her own name was called. A few of the names were familiar to her by reputation, but the majority were not. When Mr. Maguire finished his list it appeared that all were present, for Mr. Murray got to his feet once more and said, "It is a good beginning to have you all here on time. I want it kept up. A stock company is no place for late arrivals. Those of you who are experienced will know what I mean. Joe will give out the principal sides now and tomorrow at ten sharp I want the first reading. We'll cast the minor roles at that time also. That's all."

A babble of conversation broke out immediately after the manager stopped speaking. Mr. Maguire and Mark were circulating among the principals, handing them their parts, or "sides."

Nan slid off the window sill, feeling out of it, until the boy next to her said, "Well, that's that."

Nan nodded. "What do we do now?" she asked.

He grinned. "An hour ago I would have said, sleep. But now I'm wide awake and no place to go, to paraphrase."

Nan and the girl Mark had introduced as Helen Graves smiled at his sally.

"You at least know someone in the company," the girl said, apparently referring to Mark, and added, "Where are you living?"

"With friends," Nan answered, "and you?"

The girl shrugged. "At a boarding house," she said, and Nan gathered she was not too crazy about it.

"Let's all go and have some coffee, shall we?" Bud Parks suggested.

Nan giggled. "I'd love to, except for the fact that I don't know my way home and Mark has promised to take me. I'm afraid I'll have to wait for him."

"O.K. Be seeing you tomorrow then. Coming, Helen?" Bud asked and the two of them moved off, leaving Nan alone.

During their conversation the room had slowly emptied and now there were only a few people in it. Una Fair and Hartley Bennett had gone. Nan did not see Alicia around either, so she simply stood where she was and waited for Mark to come over to her. At last he did so, followed by Joe Maguire.

"Mr. Maguire," Mark said, "this is my friend, Nan Lane, whom I told you about."

"Glad to meet you, Nan," Mr. Maguire said and consulted one of his lists, which Nan was to discover he never seemed to be without. "Are you all settled? Got a room?"

"I am staying with friends," Nan explained once more. To her surprise, Mr. Maguire frowned.

"Well, I don't know. You are listed as a student. We've just five of you this year, and we are responsible for seeing that you are properly placed. There's nothing here about your being with friends. Says you should be at the Shirley Arms. It is one of the approved places here."

Nan tried to explain.

"I *was* at the Shirley Arms at first, but my mother got in touch with a friend of hers and I'm staying at her house instead. Isn't that all right?"

Mr. Maguire sighed, in the manner of a much overburdened person being confronted with still another problem.

"If your mother knows the people, I suppose it will be all right, but we'll have to have their names and address. Matter of fact, I'll probably have to get in touch with them."

"Their name is Stockton—Mr. and Mrs. James Stockton of—" and Nan gave the address.

To her surprise, Mr. Maguire's manner changed entirely.

"Oh, the James Stocktons! Well, that's fine—just fine!" He beamed upon Nan much as had the house mother at the Shirley Arms when Mrs. Stockton had taken her away from there.

"You'll be well taken care of there, no need for *me* to worry. See you tomorrow then. Now Mark, I'd like to have you to help me with the sets."

Nan broke in hastily, "Mr. Maguire, may Mark take me to the bus first? I know it sounds silly, but I was driven here today and I've no idea how to get home."

Mr. Maguire laughed, actually laughed. "Put the girl on her bus, Mark, if you know which one it is."

"The chauffeur told him," Nan said seriously.

Mr. Maguire seemed even more amused at this.

"Run along then, and get back here pronto, young Mark. I didn't know you had connections."

It was Mark's turn to be bewildered.

"I haven't," he said. "I only know Nan—and the chauffeur."

"Well, in this town it won't hurt you a bit to make the acquaintance of her hosts," Mr. Maguire remarked drily as he turned to leave them.

"Come along," Mark said abruptly.

Meekly, Nan followed him, back through the darkened theater, past the doorman and out into the sunshine. Mark turned purposefully down the street, walking so fast that Nan almost had to run to keep up with him.

"Mark," she protested at last, as he stalked on in complete silence. "Mark, I can't walk so fast."

"I'm sorry, Nan." He scowled, but slowed his pace. "The bus stop is right over there. That chauffeur said you take a #12 and stay on it until you reach your street. You can see the house from the Avenue."

"Mark," Nan asked, "just who are the Stocktons?"

Mark stared at her as if she had taken leave of her senses.

"No, really—I mean, who *are* they in this town? Mr. Maguire certainly knew them and was impressed."

"I have no idea, except that obviously they have money. Not every one has a chauffeur, you know, or perhaps *your* friends all have."

"Mark, I wish you wouldn't sound like that!" Nan was close to tears. "It's hardly fair. You've been to my house —you know my family. Why shouldn't my mother know people with money. Surely it's not a crime? Mrs. Stockton has been lovely to me and I think you'd like them if you knew them. Instead, you act this way—" Her voice failed her.

"I'm sorry, Nan. It wasn't right of me to take it out on you—it's no fault of yours. But I'd rather hoped I'd see a lot of you while we were out here and now I guess all your time will be spent with your new friends."

"No it won't, Mark, truly. Oh, I know Mrs. Stockton will want me to go about with them occasionally; but, after all, I came here for the theater and I want to be with theater people."

By now they had reached the bus stop and stood there as Nan finished speaking. Wistfully she added, "We've not talked a bit about this morning and there were so many questions I wanted to ask you."

"I'm sorry, Nan," Mark repeated. "It's just that I can't compete with money."

"But *I* haven't got any money!" Nan protested vehemently.

What Mark would have replied was lost as the bus drew

up and Nan boarded it. She paid her fare, asked the driver to let her know when she reached her street and sat down, fuming inwardly.

She didn't know whether to be angrier at Mark or the Stocktons. Between them, they had thoroughly spoiled the day which should have been so exciting.

Still, it was nice, and rather surprising, to know that Mark was so interested in her. He'd never before actually said anything which she could hug to herself, as she could now hug the thought that he wanted to see a great deal of her. Her pleasure in his remarks was lessened, naturally, by his very sureness that she would be a willing captive to her hosts. Well, Nan determined, she just would not let that happen.

11

Decisions

NAN SPENT a restless evening and night. Mrs. Stockton had kindly suggested that they might go to a movie together, a suggestion which Nan had courteously, but firmly, declined.

Her excuse that she was tired after the excitement of the first day was not the entire truth. The truth of the matter was that she was not anxious to have the Stocktons put her too deeply in their debt. She wanted to establish in her own mind what her attitude toward them was to be.

It was unthinkable that, after their great kindness to her, she could simply leave and go back to the residence club; nor did she really wish to do so.

Instinctively, Nan realized that her living with them might well affect the attitudes of other members of the company toward her. It had already affected Mark and Mr. Maguire. Even Helen Graves, who seemed to dislike her own rooming house so much had reacted to Nan's remark that she was living with friends. It would set her apart and, even more so, as there was no doubt that the Stocktons were important in this town and Nan had no desire to cling to their coattails. She had her own place to make and she wanted to make it without help.

In the living room after supper, while Mr. and Mrs. Stockton drank their after-dinner coffee, Nan was subjected to a variety of questions about her day.

"No," she said in answer to one, "I haven't a part as yet and I'm not even sure there are small parts to be had in this play they're doing. However, I understand that, whether I have a part or not, I will be expected to be on hand for all the rehearsals—just to observe and to learn."

"I'm afraid that would seem pretty dull to me," Mrs. Stockton confessed. "However, I suppose when you are bitten by the stage bug, rehearsals are interesting, whether you have a part or not. Tell me, did you see the young people you know? The boy and the girl you were telling me about?"

"Yes, though I didn't have a chance to speak to Alicia. Mark showed me around and he put me on the bus to come home. He had to go back to work on the settings. He is the assistant stage manager, you know."

Mrs. Stockton smiled. "Oh, then he's working with Joe Maguire."

"Why, yes, he is. Do you know Mr. Maguire?" Nan was surprised. It had never occurred to her that Mr. Maguire might know Mrs. Stockton, personally.

"Yes, indeed. We went to high school together. Joe always had the stage bug. He used to manage all our shows at school."

Nan breathed an inner sigh of relief. So *that* was all Mr. Maguire's ready acceptance of her change in residence had meant! He knew Mrs. Stockton.

Mrs. Stockton's next remark, however, put Nan right back into the frame of mind that had troubled her, for her hostess went on to say, "Jim and I are stockholders in the company and we generally give a dinner for the cast out

at the club, before the season is over. Now that we have
a member of the company living in our own home, though,
I think it would be nice if we gave some small luncheons
for your friends."

"Oh, no!" Nan exclaimed involuntarily. "Please don't
do that! I mean, it would look as if I were trying to curry
favor."

"She's right." Mr. Stockton spoke quietly. "It doesn't
do for a member of the working force to even seem to be
currying favor with the administration. The theater is no
different from business in that respect."

Nan flashed him a grateful look.

"I do thank you all the same," she said earnestly, "but
you are doing quite enough for me as it is. It's nice to be
in a home and I just love Sue's room."

Mrs. Stockton seemed not in the least offended and
merely shrugged off the rebuff with, "Well, no luncheons,
if you say so—though I think it's silly to feel that way. I
do want you to feel free to bring your friends here if you
like, however. Remember, it is your home, too, at least for
this summer."

"I know—and I will," Nan promised.

After that, the subject changed but Nan's mind kept going over the whole matter and, as a result, she spent a restless night. She was in a position that required tact, and it
was made no easier by the fact that she liked the Stocktons
so much.

Nan was wakened by her alarm clock in the morning,
dressed carefully, ate a good breakfast (over which she told
Annie all about the first day in the theater) and went cheerfully off to the bus to attend the ten o'clock rehearsal. In
the daylight, her problems seemed much simpler.

She had made up her mind on two courses of action and to these she meant to stick.

First, she would try some time very soon to make Mark understand her position for what it was. Also, she would try to see that he met the Stocktons at the earliest opportunity. She had decided that Mrs. Stockton was her own best salesman.

Second, and as a test, she wanted Alicia to find out with whom she was staying. If Alicia, as a result, became overfriendly, she would know whether her fears were justified. Common sense told her that Alicia had not been in town long enough to know who the Stocktons really were, but give her a few days, and Nan intended that she should find out.

With all this settled in her mind, Nan went blithely to the theater, greeted Mr. Mac like an old friend, looked dutifully at the notice board and went on into the greenroom.

Bud Parks and Helen Graves were once more perched on the window sill and Nan made her way over to them. They welcomed her and made a place for her. Nan looked about, spotted Mark, waved to him and was glad when he waved back, though he did not come over.

Before the hour set for rehearsal, everyone except the stars, Mr. Murray and Alicia were present. At ten sharp Mr. Murray arrived, followed almost immediately by Hartley Bennett, Una Fair and, almost on their heels, Alicia.

It was, Nan realized, perfect timing. Alicia was not late—but she had come at a time when she was sure to be noticed. Unconcerned, apparently, and looking remote and lovely, Alicia found an empty chair and sat down. Shortly afterward, the role was called and rehearsal got under way.

Nan was surprised to find that the first reading was actually just that—a reading. Everyone remained seated and, at a word from Mr. Murray, the principals opened their "sides." Briefly Mr. Murray described the setting of the first act—then he said, "Curtain," and immediately sat down at his small table, as he had the day before, and seemed to lose all interest in the proceedings while the cast read their parts.

Nan was surprised to find that none of the principals made the least attempt to "act" their lines. They simply read, somewhat monotonously. Mr. Murray, however, seemed satisfied. The entire first act was gone through in this manner and a part of the second, with Mark reading aloud the small parts that had not yet been assigned.

About the middle of the second act, Mr. Murray glanced at his watch and rose. Everyone instantly stopped reading. "Lunch," he announced. "Back in three quarters of an hour. Joe, come here."

As Nan slid off the window seat, Bud asked, "Where are you going to eat?"

"Mark and I had coffee across the street yesterday, in the drugstore. Do you suppose we could get sandwiches there?"

"Perhaps—or there's a little restaurant around the corner where I ate yesterday," Helen offered.

"Let's try that; I'm hungry," Bud suggested.

Nan saw Mark off to one side and saying, "Be with you in a sec'," went over to him. "Mark, I'm going out to lunch with Bud and Helen. Do you want to come along?"

"I'd like to, but I'm not sure whether Mr. Maguire will need me. You go ahead and I'll follow if I can. Where are you eating?"

"Helen says there's a little restaurant around the corner, she's eaten there. I don't even know the name of the place."

Mark nodded. "Burt's," he told her. "Most of the cast eat there. O.K. I'll be along if I can."

Not a remark about yesterday, but no special warmth in his tone either, Nan thought, as she rejoined Helen and Bud.

The "little restaurant" turned out to be a regular coffee-pot place, with a counter down one side and about six white-topped tables.

Four of the tables were already occupied by members of the stock company. It seemed to Nan at a first hasty glance that everyone was there except the principals and Alicia.

The restaurant's one waitress was scurrying about, flustered at having so many customers at once. Several members of the company evidently knew her and they bantered with her good-naturedly.

"Well," Helen asked, as the three of them sat down and picked up their menus, "what did you think of the first rehearsal?"

"To tell you the truth, I was surprised," Nan replied. "In dramatic school, we were always supposed to learn our parts before the rehearsal."

"Where did you go to school? Mark told me, but I've forgotten."

"Booth School, New York," Nan answered, not without pride.

"One of the best in the country," Bud commented, then added, "Though I don't believe any of them—dramatic schools, I mean—really prepare you for the stage."

Nan was genuinely shocked. "What makes you say that? Loads of our best actors and actresses have come from dramatic schools."

"Oh, I know that! Sure, they teach you voice control, poise, make-up—all sorts of techniques. No, what I mean is they don't give you the real atmosphere. They can't, of course. Like your being surprised at the first reading. Tell me truly, Nan, after listening to those professionals reading today, would you say they'd be ready to put on that play next week?"

Nan flushed as she replied, "Frankly, no."

Bud laughed at her honest answer. "That's what I mean. When you become a professional, you learn pace and timing. You become what is known as a 'quick study.' In other words, that flat, uninteresting reading took root today *inside* those people and in a few days they'll know all the words and will have grown into the parts without seeming to try."

"All of them?" Nan asked.

Bud smiled. "Well, maybe not all," he conceded, "but most. That's the way it works."

"Have you been in the theater long yourself?" Nan asked, interested.

"My parents were theatrical. Never really made the big time; except for small parts now and then, but they played all over the sticks. It's a hard life and they tried to keep me from it. Used to settle me down with my grandparents and go off. Once or twice, though, for one reason and another, they took me along and I loved it." Bud sighed. "Mom's dead now," he said, "and Dad's playing Boston. Got him to let me come out here. He's hoping I won't like it—but of course I do."

"Then you haven't had any training?"

"Nope, none," Bud answered cheerfully.

"And you?" Nan asked Helen.

"Dramatic school, like yourself, but one not so well known as yours, I'm afraid. In Cleveland. This is my second year in stock, however."

"I feel like a real novice beside the two of you! So, if I do or say something dreadful, you'll help me out, won't you?" Nan asked.

Both of her companions raised their right hands, palm outwards, "We swear," they said solemnly, then all of them laughed.

"Here comes the waitress, at last. What'll it be?" Bud asked.

Hamburger, French fries, coffee and ice cream was the unanimous choice and Mark came in just in time to make it four of the same.

12

A Dressing Down

ON HER WAY HOME following the afternoon rehearsal, Nan reflected that there was one nice thing about living with a family, you were sure you had someone at home with whom you could talk over the events of the day.

It had been a full day, a revealing day, for Nan, but most of all she was full of one incident that had taken place at the beginning of the afternoon reading. It was this which she could hardly wait to describe to Mr. and Mrs. Stockton that night at the supper table, although she managed to hold off until Mrs. Stockton asked the inevitable question: "Well, Nan, how did the day go?"

"Oh, Mrs. Stockton, it was so interesting! Una Fair is to be the star and we are producing *The Girl of the Golden West* and Hartley Bennett is the leading man. They read their parts today, but Bud Parks (he's one of the students) said that by tomorrow they'll begin to really act them. I had lunch with Bud and Helen Graves and Mark. But the thing I'm dying to tell you about is something awful that happened to Alicia. In the morning she came into the rehearsal room right after the stars. She was actually the last person to arrive and she took a chair right near them. I didn't think anything about it one way or another at that

79

time; but after lunch, when we came back, she was already in the room and she was sitting on the sofa where Miss Fair and Mr. Bennett had sat before. They weren't back yet. When Mark saw her he said, 'I do hope she'll get up from there before the stars come back.' Bud, who doesn't know Alicia, said, 'Oh, of course she will.' I think Mark might have gone over and spoken to her then, except that Mr. Maguire came and took him away. So when Mr. Murray and the stars came back, it was awful!"

Nan paused, and Mrs. Stockton asked, "What was awful? Don't keep us in suspense!"

"Well, Bud and Helen and myself shoved up onto the window seat again. I did sort of wonder why we couldn't sit on chairs, too, though actually the window seat is wide and it's always cool there. Anyway, when Miss Fair and Mr. Bennett came in, they went right over to the sofa and Alicia gave them what Mark calls her 'Mona Lisa' smile and moved over to one side. Anyone could see that it was a tight fit—Miss Fair is not *stout*, but she's not slim either—"

Mrs. Stockton nodded in agreement. "Go on," she prompted.

"Mr. Murray had gone over to the table where he sits and he had turned his back to the sofa, but when he sat down he was facing it again. He riffled through all those papers he has on his table and then he looked up and, honestly, I've never seen anyone madder! He stared and his face kept getting redder and redder and finally he roared out so loud that everyone stopped talking, 'Who in heavens name are you?' No one answered and everyone looked at everyone else and didn't seem to know what he was talking about. Truthfully, I thought he'd taken leave of his senses! Then he slapped his palm down hard on the table and stood up. 'You there, on the sofa, who are you?' he demanded.

" 'Now Stew . . .' Miss Fair began, but he didn't let her finish. He repeated again, 'Who are you?' and pointed his finger right at Alicia.

"Alicia did look a little pale, but when she spoke she seemed cool enough. 'My name is Alicia Van Delyss, if that's what you mean,' she said.

" 'Well then, let's put it this way, Miss Van Delyss. Who do you *think* you are?'

"Alicia didn't answer that, and Miss Fair put her hand out as if to stop Mr. Murray, but he walked right over to the sofa. 'I'll tell you who you are, Miss Van Delyss. You are a bit player in this company. You'll act like it, beginning *now*. Get up off that sofa and take a chair—sit on the floor—stand on your head—I don't care what you do, except *don't ever again* try to suck up to the stars. Yes, I noticed you yesterday, trailing us in—yes, I noticed you today at luncheon, at the table next to ours in the hotel. That, Miss Van Delyss, is *not* the way to attract attention.'

"There was dead silence for a minute and then Alicia got up, moved over to a chair and sat down in her graceful way, and the rehearsal began. It was awful!" Nan finished with a reminiscent shudder.

"I should think so—but I quite see Mr. Murray's point. From what you've told me about this girl, she must be pretty unbearable," Mrs. Stockton said. "Maybe this will do her some good."

Nan shrugged and looked puzzled. "I don't know," she confessed. "Alicia is a very funny mixture. I was feeling sorry for her myself, so after the rehearsal broke up, I went over to her and told her I thought Mr. Murray had been pretty hard on her. Do you know what she said? She said it didn't matter a bit, because now everyone knew who she was! Then she said she bet she'd get a part when the tryouts begin tomorrow. 'There's only one female part besides the lead, and I'm going to get it!' she announced. Then, sweet as butter, she asked me how the 'Sheltering Arms' was. Honest! She actually called it that and I bet she did it on purpose. She made it sound just like an orphanage!"

Mrs. Stockton laughed so heartily at this and at her young guest's aggrieved manner that Nan had to pause a minute before she could go on. "She makes me so mad! But, do you know, I don't think she was really very happy. Only I'll bet she's right about getting the part she wants. She has her heart set on it and she's a very good actress."

"Altogether somewhat of an enigma, your Alicia," Mrs. Stockton remarked. "I'd like to meet her some time, though. She sounds interesting."

"Maybe I'll bring her around some day, but she's an awful pusher," Nan warned her hostess.

"I wonder why?" Mrs. Stockton mused. "From what you say, she has money and background. I would think it more likely that someone like Mark might be the pusher."

"Mercy, no!" Nan exclaimed. "He almost disowned me that first day when I drove up in a chauffeur-driven car and told him I wasn't staying at the residence club."

Mr. Stockton chuckled. "Margaret lives in a very small world," he said. "She'd be surprised if she met all the different types I meet every day in business. The pushers, the secure, the sly, the lazy and odd combinations of all of them —such as Miss Van Delyss seems to be."

Mrs. Stockton bridled. "I can't help it if my world is small, Jim. I'm perfectly willing to be taught and I think that this summer, with Nan here, I'm going to enlarge it a lot. That is, if Nan will ever bring her friends here, as I've asked her to."

Catching the wistfulness in Mrs. Stockton's voice, Nan said impulsively, "I'll bring them all, if they'll come, Mrs. Stockton, Alicia especially!"

"That's fine and Nan, I do wish you'd be less formal with me. How about calling me Aunt Peggy?"

"I'd like to, thank you—Aunt Peggy," Nan replied.

It did not at all surprise Nan that Alicia secured the part she had set her heart on. No sensible director, no matter how he felt personally, could overlook the fact that both by type and voice she suited the part, as Nan reported to the Stocktons the next day.

"You make me more and more curious about this girl," Mrs. Stockton said. And again Nan promised that she would see that they met. But she was to meet Alicia much sooner and under quite different circumstances from any she had pictured.

By the middle of the week the play was being acted and, except for occasional lapses, the leads knew their lines, as Bud had predicted they would. On Thursday, the whole action was played out on a bare stage. On Friday, the props were there. Saturday, there was a full rehearsal, but without make-up or costumes.

Mr. Murray was dissatisfied with several spots in the play and he went over them again and again, turning a three-hour play into a good seven hours, so everyone was exhausted when it was over.

"Sunday, 5 P.M.—Dress Rehearsal." The notice on the bulletin board read, when Nan left at 5:30 on Saturday.

She was dead tired and her head ached, but after a hot bath and a half-hour rest she felt much better and had just begun to dress for dinner when a knock came at her door.

"Come in," she called.

Mrs. Stockton poked her head into the room. "Put on a nice frock, dear. We are going to the club for dinner—" Nan opened her mouth to say she was too tired—and closed it again. She was not really that tired now and all week she had stuck at home—besides, the rehearsal wasn't until five tomorrow. She'd get a good sleep before then and it would be fun to see the friends she had met at the club before.

Nan lost a part of what Mrs. Stockton was telling her as these thoughts ran through her head. She came to in time to hear Mrs. Stockton say, "—so I took a table and there'll be Sally and Jud, and you and Roger Tyler, besides Jim and myself."

"That's nice—thank you. Shall I wear this, or this, do you think?" Nan asked, going to the closet and bringing out two dresses.

While Mrs. Stockton considered the dresses critically, her head on one side, Nan thought, "And who is Roger Tyler? I don't dare ask, for I should have been listening. Oh, well, if he's as nice as Sally and Jud and Mary Riner, I needn't worry."

Mrs. Stockton made her choice of the dresses (a choice which happily coincided with Nan's own) and the latter began to dress, already looking forward with pleasure to the evening ahead.

13

Surprise Evening

IT WAS CLOSE TO DUSK when the Stocktons' car turned off the highway onto the country club road. The tires hissed at the sudden change from smooth macadam to a graveled surface.

"Sounds like the swish of a rain squall against a window-pane, doesn't it?" Mr. Stockton asked.

"It does at that!" Nan exclaimed appreciatively.

The remark was the first one Mr. Stockton had made on the way out, although his wife and Nan had chatted continuously about one thing and another. Mr. Stockton, Nan was discovering, did not say much, as a rule, but when he did, it was apt to be something worthwhile. Nan sat quietly now and listened to the rhythm of the tires until they drove into the parking lot. A great many cars were there already and, in the gathering dusk, gay voices came from the lighted clubhouse.

The band was playing inside, and its catchy tune set Nan's feet into a little impromptu dance step as she got out of the car.

While the three were walking toward the wide, lighted veranda, however, the little flutter of nervousness centering in her stomach which often accompanied any new experience went through Nan like a small, chill wind, and as quickly she shrugged it off.

"I don't see—" Mrs. Stockton began, and then, "oh, yes. There they are! Jud, Sally, Roger, have you been waiting long?"

Three figures detached themselves from a group and came toward them. Jud and Sally greeted Nan as an old friend, and then Mrs. Stockton introduced Roger.

A little to Nan's disappointment, he turned out to be a medium tall, spectacled young man, a little older than the others.

"Nan, this is Roger Tyler," Mrs. Stockton said. "Roger, I'd like to have you meet Nan Lane, the daughter of a very dear friend of mine. Nan is spending the summer with us."

Hands were shaken and the usual comments made and then they all moved together toward the club dining room.

It wasn't until they were seated that Mrs. Stockton said, "Nan, Roger is interested in the theater, too—as a playwright. That is why I thought you might enjoy each other."

Nan was relieved to see that Roger looked as embarrassed as she felt, when he replied, "Miss Lane, I'm not even a budding playwright, yet, I do assure you. It is true that it is my chief interest. I majored in drama and I hope some day to write for the theater. Right now, though, I'm selling insurance—rather slowly."

Nan liked him immediately for his humility.

"I'm not much farther along the road," she admitted candidly. "I don't even have a walk-on part as yet. I'm wishing hard for next week, though, when they cast a new play."

Further conversation was suspended until the orders for

dinner were given. Then Jud asked Sally to dance and Roger rose to ask Nan.

To her delight, Roger was a very smooth dancer. He held her neither too close, nor too loosely, and their steps matched perfectly. Nor, save for an occasional comment or question, did he try to talk as they danced. It was very satisfactory and by the time the last bar had been played and they had made their way back to the table, the last trace of Nan's nervousness had vanished and she was very hungry.

Supper was gay, with the conversation general, and Nan was thoroughly enjoying herself when a couple entered the room and sat down two tables away. Nan could not help staring, for the girl was Alicia. Dressed in dramatic black and white, with deep eye-shadow and scarlet lips, she drew many eyes to her. Accompanying her was Mr. Torley, of the train!

Something must have been said to Nan which she failed to catch, for she suddenly became aware of a silence at her table.

"I—I'm sorry," she stammered, in some confusion. "I just saw someone I know come in. Mrs. Stockton, that girl over at the table on the left is Alicia, and the man with her is someone I—er—met on the train—Mr. Torley."

Under his breath Jud gave an expressive whistle and Sally glanced sharply at him.

"Looks like an actress, doesn't she?" Jud said hastily.

Nan laughed. "Well she is! In the regular company. She graduated from my dramatic school this year."

"You simply must introduce her to me later," Mrs. Stockton said.

Nan promised to do so and the conversation went on to other matters.

However, Nan could not help an occasional glance in the direction of the other table, and she caught two bits of pantomime that needed no words.

Alicia saw her, nodded coolly and then obviously pointed her out to Mr. Torley. He, in his turn, being sideways to their table, turned to bow to her, took a long look at the other occupants of the table and began to talk earnestly to Alicia. As he leaned forward, Nan could almost hear him. When her eyes again caught Alicia's the cool look was replaced by a brilliant smile that said, "See, I'm your friend. Remember me, do."

The change was sudden, not unexpected, but, as always with Alicia, somehow disappointing. It was as if somewhere in this girl Nan always expected to find something more real, less obvious and calculating—though why, she could not have said.

Later in the evening, in the ballroom, Nan did introduce Alicia and Mr. Torley to her companions. Mr. Torley immediately attached himself, with some firmness, to Mr. Stockton. Alicia, on the other hand, was so charming to Mrs. Stockton as to quite disarm Nan. Somehow she had expected Alicia to show her preference for the men of the party.

It wasn't until Jud asked Alicia to dance, and Roger asked Sally, that Nan found herself seated alone beside Mrs. Stockton. Mr. Torley and Mr. Stockton were too deep in a conversation to notice them.

"So that is the fabulous Alicia? She's just as attractive, just as brash and probably just as talented as you painted her, my dear."

Nan was completely amazed. "Why—why—I thought she acted very well. I mean, frankly, I thought she'd make a set for Jud and not be so nice to you—" Nan flushed. "I don't mean anyone wouldn't be nice to you, but—"

"But not Alicia?" Mrs. Stockton finished for her. "You misjudge the girl's shrewdness. Mr. Torley is well known to my husband. They've had some business dealings. Alicia is far too young a girl to be going about alone with a man of his age and type. She wouldn't, if she knew someone younger and more eligible. Now she sees a way, but that way is not to fling herself at Jud (though he'd likely be her choice) but rather to get to know me."

"Oh, I see," Nan murmured, although actually it was all still rather vague to her. Her mind simply did not work that way and suddenly, for all the good time she'd had and the attention of a really nice college man, she wished Mark were along.

To Mark, black was black and white was white. He was restful. I must see more of him, she thought. Subtleties were not for her.

14

Dreams

Sunday nan wakened in time for church and ate a solitary breakfast afterwards, as the Stocktons had not yet come down. After breakfast, she decided to forego the Sunday papers, for the time, and write to a few of her friends at home.

She had already written to her mother and her grandmother several times and minutely described the theater and the people connected with it, as well as the Stocktons and their warm hospitality.

Now, however, writing to Betty, she really began to express all the many strange personal problems that confronted her.

"—It seems as if I am living in two, or maybe three, separate worlds and it is a little hard to feel easy about it," she wrote. "You remember Mark, don't you? Well, I'd rather thought he'd be the only friend I had out here. He is a nice boy, though I'm not a bit sentimental about him, but he has gone all stuffy since I've moved in with the Stocktons."

So Nan wrote on and on, taking no account of the time, but unburdening herself of all her confusions. Her doubts, still persistent, about the theater as a career, her liking for the good times at the country club, and yet her knowledge that she must not become involved with them, if she was to be in earnest about her work.

When she finally brought the letter to a close, she sat quietly for a long time, simply staring into space. At last she picked the letter up, read it through, shrugged and, tearing it into small pieces, consigned it to the wastebasket. It wouldn't interest Betty a bit, she knew, but it had curiously relieved her of tension. With a wry smile at herself, she took up her pen and scribbled a few crisp paragraphs to Betty, mostly about the club, affixed a stamp to the accompanying envelope and went out to find a postbox.

The day was so nice that she walked for several blocks, enjoying the sight of well tended lawns and flower-filled gardens. When she got back it was past one o'clock and the Stocktons, who had been back from church for some time, had begun to worry.

The rest of the afternoon was occupied by a hearty dinner, a nap and a bath and then Mr. Stockton drove her to the theater in time for rehearsal. She could not give him even an approximate time to call for her, as she had no idea when the dress rehearsal would be over. She did promise that, if it was very late, she'd get someone to walk her to the bus.

As a matter of fact, the rehearsal, once underway, went off very quickly. It was neither good, nor notably bad. Most of the difficulties were technical. A dozen times, or more, a halt was called while lights were adjusted or some property changed. It was tedious and not at all thrilling— just hard work.

When Alicia made a point of coming over to talk to her, Nan was not surprised.

"It's too bad there are no walk-ons or bit parts for girls in this show," she said.

"You needn't worry, you got the one part there was. And I do wish you luck in it," Nan replied briefly.

Alicia shrugged and changed the subject.

"Wasn't it funny, my meeting you out at the club? I just happened to run into Mr. Torley and I was hot and bored, so I accepted his invitation. I didn't know you had friends out here—you never told me."

"I did tell you; but I don't think you paid any attention to it at the time. They are friends of my mother's and I never met them before I came here, but I am spending the summer with them. I expect I'll see you at the club again. We go out there often."

Nan couldn't resist the small brag, though she felt decidedly uncomfortable after having delivered it, but Alicia merely said, "I expect so," and dropped the subject.

After rehearsal, Nan found Mark waiting for her.

"Anyone calling for you?" he asked.

"No, Mr. Stockton offered to, but I couldn't tell him when rehearsal would be over, so I said I'd take the bus home. They tend to worry over me."

"I'll treat you to coffee and take you home, then. O.K.?" Mark asked.

"Love to."

In the drugstore, Mark said, "I'm sorry I acted so silly the other day, Nan. I guess I'd counted on being the one to 'worry over you,' as you put it. Really though, I'm glad that you are with good friends, even though I suppose it will mean I'll see less of you than I'd hoped."

"It needn't, Mark, unless you want it so. The Stocktons are wonderful people and they'll want to take me about some, of course—like last night, when we went to the Country Club. But I've made up my mind that I must stick to the theater crowd more. As it is, I'm uncertain about my future, really. I feel I want the theater as a career but I'm timid about my own abilities. On the other hand, unless I really stick to the theater and the people and stop dividing myself, I'll never find out, will I?"

"What would you do if you decided against the stage?" Mark asked curiously.

Nan looked helpless. "I've really no idea. What about yourself, you told me once you had ideas and I gathered they didn't include the professional theater. Just what are they?"

Mark's whole face lit up, "I'm glad you asked me," he said and leaned forward to grasp her hand. "I did so hope you'd want to know. What I would like to do is to work with children, in dramatics."

"You mean to teach?"

"No, though perhaps there'd have to be a certain amount of that first. My idea is to found a real theater for children —a theater which would have the best quality acting available, but which would deal with scripts suitable for children. I know how much the performances I saw as a child affected me. I know, too, how often the best is not possible for people with little money."

"How about TV? They do a great many children's programs."

"I know they do and I'm not belittling them. Some of them are very good, but to my mind there is nothing that takes the place of the feeling between the actor and the live audience. How is the theater to exist if children no longer are able to see good plays? In the old days, there was some form of the drama in almost every small town. So, that's my great idea."

"Mark, it's a wonderful idea. I can just see you making good with it, too."

"Nan! Maybe some time you could help me with it. We might have a real traveling theater for children—" Mark stopped and then added soberly, "That dream is for the future. I've not a cent of money to get started with and I'll need a lot more experience than I've had to attract anyone else to invest in the idea."

"But you can work toward it, Mark. You must learn all that you possibly can about stage management this summer, and meanwhile, I'll try my best to make a real success of acting; or at least of observing, for so far that's all I've done! Who knows, some day we might be able to team up. Next to the theater, I do love children. You've no idea how I've always envied big families like yours!"

Mark laughed. "They are fun and I think the older you get, the more you realize it. Anyway, we'll both do our best and, if the future finds us together in my dream, we can always remember when and where we first talked about it. Meanwhile, don't overdo this country club stuff, will you?"

Nan laughed. "No, I won't. But I want you to meet the Stocktons. You're bound to like them, and they'll like you, too."

They finished their coffee and walked to the bus and on the way home Nan told Mark about Alicia and the Stocktons at the Country Club. She told him, too, of the nice young people she had met there—of Sally Holly and her desire to act, of Roger Tyler and his ambitions. She could see that to him this presented a new aspect of people with money.

"I don't know," he said thoughtfully. "I never believed anything was barred to you, if you had the money."

Nan shook her head. "That's not so," she said. "There are lots of barred doors that only talent and study, or perseverance, can open, and they're just as hard for the person with money to enter; sometimes harder."

Mark grinned. "Guess I've a lot to learn this summer, too," he said.

"I'm quite sure you have," Nan told him serenely, "and I intend to teach you!"

When they arrived at the house, Nan was glad to find the Stocktons in and alone. They welcomed Mark cordially and presently had him entirely at his ease, as they asked him about his work at the theater.

Before he left, Mrs. Stockton said, "Jim and I will be at the opening tomorrow and we wish you the best of luck. Won't you join Nan and ourselves for a midnight snack after the show?"

"I'd like to, thank you," Mark replied. "See you tomorrow then, Nan. Good night—and again my thanks."

"He's a very nice boy, Nan," Mrs. Stockton said, after he had left. "Would you by any chance be *specially* interested in him?"

"No! Oh, no! We're just good friends—but he is nice. Night."

Nan fled to her room.

Was she specially interested?

Truthfully, she didn't know. Until she had come out here, Mark had been just another boy she enjoyed being with. Yet without a word being said, until his outburst of this evening (and *that* was hardly sentimental), she had known he was fond of her. Was she growing fond of him?

She tried to analyze her feelings and failed. All she knew was that she was happy that their brief estrangement was over, happy that her hosts liked him—and he them, she was pretty sure. Happy—happy—she thought and drifted into sleep.

15

First Night

To NAN IT SEEMED as if that long Monday would never end. The day was a lovely one and she knew she had only to say so and she might go swimming at the pool, or for a drive, but she did not want these things.

A strange restlessness possessed her. At last, on impulse, she went to the phone and called Mark at the number he had given her, only to learn that he was out. Of course, he would be at the theater, Nan realized. She tried to settle down with a book and could not keep her mind on the printed page.

Mrs. Stockton came to her door about ten-thirty, to ask if she would care to go downtown with her to do some shopping. Nan refused politely.

When Mrs. Stockton had left, however, she wished she had gone with her hostess. Another half-hour of agonizing inactivity and Nan suddenly made up her mind.

She would take the bus and drop in at Burt's, perhaps some of the cast would be there. She felt an urgent need to be with them. Leaving word with Annie that she would be back in time for dinner, she started off.

To her delight, when she arrived at the restaurant she found that Bud, Helen, Peggy Worth and several of the others were there. They waved their welcome to her and she went over to their table. Lanky Bud got up and dragged over another chair for her.

"What brings you in here?" he asked. "Not that we aren't glad to see you."

Nan sat down and beamed at all of them.

"I just couldn't stay by myself all day—not today, at any rate! And I didn't want to listen to a lot of non-professional talk all day, either—so here I am. I just took a chance that you might be around." Nan interrupted herself to give her order to the waitress, who had just come up. "Coffee and a Danish, please. I had a late breakfast."

"We were just talking about tonight," Helen said. "It is always exciting here opening nights. Crowded house. Miss Fair had a cold coming on yesterday. Let's hope she licks it by tonight."

"You know, I like most of her interpretation, but in the second act, where she—" Here Peggy Worth launched into a criticism of certain aspects of Miss Fair's work. Nan listened eagerly. This was what she wanted—shop talk!

They lingered long over luncheon and then, in a companionable cluster, strolled leisurely toward a small park nearby. There, sitting in the sun, they talked endlessly of acting.

There was a sharp disagreement, entirely good-natured, between Peggy Worth and Bud. Peggy maintained that an actor had to *feel* the role to project himself entirely into it. Bud thought that a colder approach, relying mainly on *skilled technique*, created a better illusion for the audience.

Nan herself said little, being, she felt, too inexperienced, but she leaned toward Peggy's side of the argument. How long they sat there, happily absorbed, Nan had no idea, until the insistent honking of an auto horn caused Bud to stop in mid-sentence and glance toward the street.

"Nan, isn't that your friend, in the car?" he asked.

Nan followed his nod and it was indeed Mrs. Stockton.

"Goodness! I wonder how late it is," she exclaimed, conscience-stricken.

"Three-thirty," Helen replied, glancing at her watch.

"Mercy!" Peggy Worth jumped up. "And I wanted to set my hair!"

"Come over and meet Mrs. Stockton first, please do," Nan urged them.

As usual, Mrs. Stockton was unassumingly friendly and hospitable.

"Why don't you all come home with Nan?" she invited, "and have dinner before the show?"

"That's awfully nice of you, Mrs. Stockton," Peggy Worth answered, "but I've several things I must do before I go to the theater tonight. I'll come some other time, if I may?"

The others agreed that they too had commitments.

"You are welcome to come at any time," Mrs. Stockton assured them.

So Nan said good-bye and Mrs. Stockton drove her home, but the girl was relaxed now and at ease. Happily she chattered to Mrs. Stockton about the conversation in the park.

It was only as they drove into the garage and were getting out of the car that Mrs. Stockton said, somewhat wonderingly, it seemed, "All this means a great deal to you, Nan, I can see that. I was never possessed by a driving ambition, but I respect it in others. Dear, I want you to feel entirely free to go about with your friends. I'll be happy to have them here, as I've said, but perhaps you, and they, will feel more at home, well, on a park bench, shall we say? I'd not want you to regret living here; so go your own way, but once in a while let me play hostess and substitute mother."

"Of course I will!" Nan gave Mrs. Stockton an impulsive hug. "You've been so wonderful to me and I am happy here, you must know that. It is true that the theater is a sort of world apart and the more you are around it, the more absorbed you become in it. I've found that out."

Mrs. Stockton smiled and said in a thoroughly motherly tone, "Now you go take a bath and rest for a bit and then we'll have a nice light supper before we leave for the theater."

What a dear her hostess was, Nan thought, as she lay resting on her bed, I shall have to give her some of my time. Tonight, after the theater, there would be Mark and the Stocktons and herself . . . her thoughts wandered to her own mother. How she too would have loved to have been with them!

The feeling of inner excitement did not build up in Nan again until she was actually backstage. From the vantage point of the wings, where she and several other members of the company not having parts in the current production were allowed to stand, Nan could hear Mark's voice at a dressing room door. "Ten minutes to curtain." His footsteps went on to the next door and she heard him repeat the call.

Silence fell as audience and actors waited for the cue which would raise the great curtain.

Once more Mark walked his rounds. "Five minutes, on stage." Then it came, "Lights—curtain!"

Nan glanced at Miss Fair and saw that she was twisting her hands together nervously. Others were already on the set, in the positions they would hold as the curtain rose.

Distinctly Mr. Murray's voice reached them all before he ducked out of sight, into a box, stage right.

"Good luck!"

The curtain rose and Nan could see, from where she stood, about two rows of shadowy, indistinct faces, with darkness beyond. A smattering of applause began, swelled briefly and died out. The scene was the noisy interior of a barroom. The opening lines were spoken:

Sonorra: "Dooda! Dooda Day! (to the faro dealer) What did that last eight do?"

The Girl of the Golden West had begun. It was no longer a play they were doing tonight, in Metropolis—it was real. They were *living* it here. Nan watched eagerly, conscious no longer of the audience, but only of the action on the stage.

Only when the last curtain fell did she fully return to the present.

Mr. Murray, coming backstage after the curtain calls, hugged Miss Fair, kissed her roundly and said, "Good girl! How's the cold?"

"Rotten! Did you notice how I flubbed that cue in the second act?"

"Caught it nicely, though. Good work, everyone. Now, scatter and be ready for the reading of our new play tomorrow at 10:30 sharp."

It was over. Nan caught sight of Alicia, standing alone, to one side. Alicia had enjoyed a brief moment of applause for her small part, yet now, no one seemed to notice her. Nan walked over.

"Congratulations," she said. "You got applause!"

Alicia shrugged and there was something so dispirited about her that Nan said impulsively, "If you're not going somewhere else, why don't you join the Stocktons and

Mark and myself for a bite to eat—just to celebrate? Mrs. Stockton told me I was free to invite anyone I wished, at any time. They're so good to me!"

Alicia brightened up. "Why I'd like to," she said, and added, "at home I'd have scads of invitations, but out here I don't know a soul. Thanks, Nan. Wait here till I get my make-up off?"

Nan nodded, but when Mark came up to her a few minutes later he was not very happy about the invitation she had extended.

"I warned you she'll fasten on anyone she thinks can help her on and up," he said. "She could have gone out with the rest, if she'd ever taken the trouble to be friendly with them, so I don't take any stock in that lonely line of hers."

But Nan, though she often felt the same way toward Alicia, replied stubbornly, "I don't care, she looked lonely and she *did* do her part well and nobody paid her the slightest attention."

Grudgingly, Mark admitted Alicia's good work, but stuck to his point. "You know yourself that in one short week she has made herself thoroughly disliked by everyone. By the stars for her pushiness and by the rest for her aloofness."

"I know, but that made me feel even more sorry for her—" Nan began.

Mark pressed her arm, "*Sssh!* Here she comes. I hope your good deed doesn't rise up to haunt you," he said in a low voice.

The Alicia who had stood so dejectedly in the wings was not the Alicia who now came sweeping down the stairs. From her burnished dark hair to her high-heeled shoes, she was the picture of a sparklingly sophisticated young lady.

"I hope I didn't keep you waiting *too* long, Nan dear," she announced airily. "How *nice* of you to have asked Mark, too! Quite an old school reunion on our first night. Shall we go?"

There wasn't the least doubt, Nan felt now, that she had made a mistake in inviting Alicia. How patronizing could she be? She sounded as if she were conferring a favor on Nan and the Stocktons. Inside, Nan was boiling, but could think of no suitable reply. However, Mark furnished the perfect one. Very quietly he said, "Nan, if you are ready?" Placing a hand courteously on the elbow of each girl he continued, "Nan didn't ask me tonight, as a matter of fact, Mrs. Stockton did."

"Oh, I didn't know you knew her!" Alicia was startled into replying frankly, as Mark had meant her to be.

"Oh, yes." Mark's tone was casual, but he squeezed Nan's arm lightly. She squeezed back in delight and failed in her effort to repress a giggle.

"What's funny?" Alicia asked.

"Funny?" Nan echoed. "Why, nothing, really. I guess I'm just excited. Oh, there's our car. Wonder what Aunt Peggy thought of the performance?"

There, she had called Mrs. Stockton Aunt Peggy at last, and actually not for a very good motive, Nan thought ruefully. Oh, well, she'd try to make a habit of it now.

For the moment, Nan's world was wholly all right.

16

A Small Part

THE LITTLE DINNER PARTY of the night before had been very successful, after all. The Stocktons had accepted Alicia's presence with apparent pleasure, after Nan had admitted to having invited her solely on the strength of Mrs. Stockton's previous urging that she "bring her friends along, at any time."

In the same coffee shop with them were Mr. Murray, Hartley Bennett, Mr. Maguire and Peggy Worth, as well as a number of people from the audience.

Mr. Murray had come to their table with Mr. Maguire, to speak briefly to Mrs. Stockton and she in turn had told Mr. Murray that Nan was the child of one of her oldest friends, and that she was staying with her for the summer.

The director was very cordial and seemed much more friendly than he was in the theater.

It was when they were driving Alicia home, having dropped Mark off at his boarding house, that Alicia said to Nan, "It's a good thing for you that Mr. Murray saw you with your friends. Now he'll be likely to pay more attention to you."

The remark had been made to Nan alone, as Mrs. Stockton was seated up front with her husband, but Nan could feel herself flushing in the darkness, and she hoped the Stocktons had not overheard.

"Oh, I don't think he's like that—I mean, there's no reason why it should make the least bit of difference to him."

Alicia laughed knowingly. "You poor innocent!" she exclaimed. "You are staying with people who are stockholders in the company. Mr. Torley told me so. Influence and money are the most important things in life."

Even though Alicia had spoken in a low tone, Nan was in an agony for fear lest the two in the front seat should hear. Rather than start an argument, she kept still. It set very badly with her then to listen to Alicia's effusive thanks to Mrs. Stockton for her "divine evening." She wished, once more, that she'd never asked this blatant schemer along.

By the next day, however, Nan had forgotten her annoyance and was only eager to reach the theater for the new reading.

She arrived early and, having bought a paper at the corner store, was so absorbed in the review of the play that she was unaware that Mr. Murray had entered the greenroom until he spoke to her.

"Spend the night here?" he asked teasingly.

Nan smiled up at him. "Not exactly here bodily—but I do think I spent most of the night going over the play, even in my dreams," she admitted. "You see, it was my very first professional performance—if you can call watching from the wings a performance!"

"You're Nan Lane, aren't you? Well, Nan, this summer is the time for you to learn all you can about the theater. To make the most of even the smallest part assigned to you. Even when you do not have a part, I'd suggest you attend the performances, just as you attend the rehearsals. Both are important to your training. A play is like a mosaic, each part has its essential role in the whole." He stopped, ruffled his hand through his rather thin hair and grinned boyishly. "There I go, lecturing again! I was once a teacher, you know."

"I didn't know. But I will try to do as you say."

He nodded, pleased. "The reviews are good, aren't they?"

"Yes, at least this one is."

"That's what counts," he declared and left her. Nan sat thinking over what he had said and thinking, too, that, though he had called her by name, he had not mentioned last night.

As usual, the day had started out warm and by the time the full company was assembled it was hot. Everyone discussed the reviews and there was a general feeling of good will prevailing.

Nan had been so busy talking that she was not aware that Miss Fair was not there until Mr. Murray rapped for silence.

"Miss Fair is confined to her room with a bad cold, but we hope she will be able to play her role tonight. However, in case she is not well enough, I am going to assign you, Miss Graves, to understudy the part. I know your work and experience. Take the script home with you and cram. I will expect you back here at three for a brief walk-through."

Nan was thrilled, but Helen seemed to take the assignment calmly. Having received the side, she left the room unhurriedly.

A brief burst of talk rose and fell before Mr. Murray spoke again.

"This week we will rehearse *Smilin' Through*. It is quite different from the play we are doing now. Joe, will you and Mark hand out the sides? Tomorrow we will have a first reading and also tryouts for a number of bit parts. I want all of you to study the parts I'm assigning today, so that the rehearsals will go quickly after the reading. That's all."

To Nan's surprise and delight, she received a small part. It had exactly two lines, but it was a part! Of course, it made no real sense to her without a knowledge of the action within which it would be set, but that didn't matter.

At Burt's that noontime, the talk was all of Helen Graves and her good luck in being chosen as understudy.

"Though I'd not like to be in her shoes tonight—at such short notice," one member of the cast said.

For a wonder, Alicia had come into Burt's with them and now she said, "I don't think it would be such a task. After all, she has had experience. I know I could do it."

Her remark was greeted with blank silence and Nan felt a sense of embarrassment for her. Why did she always have to brag?

They all went their separate ways after coffee.

Nan was in such a happy mood that she fairly burst into the house. "I've got a part! I've got a part!" she sang and Mrs. Stockton and Annie jubilated with her, treating the thin little script as though it were a leading part.

In the afternoon, Mrs. Stockton suggested a swim and Nan was only too delighted.

"Aunt Peggy," she suggested, "could I call up Sally Holly? Perhaps she could come backstage with me one night this week. Some of the others have asked friends in for this week, so I guess it's all right."

"Why, I think that would be very nice and it's sweet of you to think of her. I like the girl and I believe there's a lot of good in her, despite her manner sometimes. She's not like your Alicia, though she may seem so on the surface."

"You don't like Alicia, do you? No one does, but do you know, Aunt Peggy, I feel sorry for her, in spite of everything. Today, when Helen was made understudy, Alicia made some remark about how easily *she* could have handled the part, and not a soul said anything!"

Mrs. Stockton nodded. "I'm afraid she's her own worst enemy. She'll not see that it is her own fault at all, or at least she'll not admit it."

"Aunt Peggy," Nan hesitated and then plunged ahead, "Alicia said the other night that, now that Mr. Murray had seen me with you, he'd pay more attention to me. Today, he did stop to speak to me and then I got this part—you don't think she's right, do you?"

Mrs. Stockton laughed and hugged Nan, "You funny child, I love you! Of course not. Naturally, when you meet someone you barely know with someone you know well, you tend to place him more easily. But I can't see Stewart Murray handing favors to anyone for such a reason. There, does that satisfy you?"

"Yes, it does," Nan admitted.

"You just go on and be yourself and you'll get all the notice you need," Mrs. Stockton assured her.

"That's exactly the way my mother talks," Nan said gratefully, then added, "I received a nice long letter from Mother today and I'll try to answer it before I go to the theater tonight. I'll call Sally now."

Sally practically came through the phone when Nan invited her to go backstage.

"You bet I'll be there! Wednesday? What time?"

"Eight o'clock sharp, so I can get you a good spot to watch from," Nan told her.

Sally shed all her brittle manner and was so grateful that Nan felt very pleased.

17

The Star Is Ill

As IT TURNED OUT, Miss Fair, though still showing signs of her cold, was on hand both Tuesday and Wednesday night.

"Aren't you horribly disappointed?" one of the students asked Helen Graves in the dressing room, where they had all congregated on Wednesday before the performance. Most of them, truthfully, were there out of curiosity, to see whether Helen or Una Fair would go on.

Helen considered the question. "No, not really. For one thing, I didn't have enough time to feel easy about the part; though I *am* word perfect. For another, the audience paid to see Miss Fair—it's her part—and for their sake and the company's, I feel better that she is able to do it."

Several of the girls nodded agreement, but Alicia said positively, "If I were you, I'd be furious! She still has a cold—you can hear it! In fact, it's worse than it was on Monday. She'll probably give a rotten performance, while you'd have a real chance."

"Una Fair doesn't give 'rotten' performances," Helen said quietly.

Sally Holly was leaning against the wall, taking in all the talk, and when she and Nan were on their way downstairs, she said suddenly, "You know I didn't like that Alicia character out at the club and I like her less now. Does she always act so superior?"

Nan nodded. "Yes," she admitted, "but she is a good actress. I have a feeling, if she'd been given the part to understudy, she'd have done very well. Yet no one likes her."

"Jud does," Sally said positively.

Nan did not have time to ask Sally how she knew this, nor what it might mean to her, for they had reached the wings.

"Stand right over here, by the prompter, and you can see everything." Nan showed Sally where to stand and crossed the empty stage to take up a position for herself.

"Lights, curtain—"

Sally was completely absorbed and Nan was glad she had brought her along. When the curtain fell at the end of the first act, Nan darted across the stage to her guest, keeping well out of the way of the stagehands.

"Miss Fair seemed as good as ever to me," she said.

"I thought so, too," Sally agreed, and added passionately, "I'd give anything to be a part of all this!"

"Maybe you will be some day," Nan encouraged her.

"When I'm ninety!" Sally replied bitterly.

Nan laughed. "I'm going up to the dressing room a minute," she said. "Do you want to stay here and watch the rest of the play, or go out front?"

"I'd rather watch it from here."

"O.K. I'll meet you on the other side, right over there, after the last curtain."

"Right, and thanks, Nan."

Nan scuttled across the stage hurriedly so she might get back in time to watch the second act. In the dressing room, she and some of the others sat and talked for a few moments.

"I'm really glad Una Fair made it," one girl said, "but she looked awful after the first act. Did you know there was a doctor in her dressing room and he gave her an injection after the curtain came down?"

Nan had not known of the doctor's presence, nor had the others, but when they heard of it, they all decided to stay until the end of the play, though only Nan and two others had been regularly attending every performance.

Very quietly, before the second act began, they slipped out into the second balcony and down the stairs until they stood, a compact and interested little group, at the back of the orchestra seats. The ushers recognized them and nodded. One of them said, in a low tone, "That Miss Fair is great! They say she's awful sick tonight."

Yet when the curtain rose, Una Fair played her hard-driving, tough Western part with all the flair they had witnessed before. As far as the little watching group could tell, she was completely herself as the curtain fell once more on the second act.

Nan and her friends spent the second act intermission outside the theater, getting a breath of air. When they went back inside, the same usher who had spoken to them before came over and, as the house lights dimmed, imparted further information. "Did you know Miss Fair fainted dead away after the last act? Fact. But they say she insists on finishing out the play."

The third act seemed to those so anxiously watching no whit different than the other two and the curtain fell to thunderous applause. But there was no curtain call. Instead, the house lights came up immediately. The audience continued clapping for a moment, stopped and hesitantly clapped again. Then, sensing something wrong, they began to gather up their things and move quietly out of the theater.

"Let's go," Nan said and quickly she and her companions ducked back of the box seats and entered the wings on the side of the stage where Nan had left Sally.

A scene of complete confusion met them. Una Fair was prostrate on the floor. A doctor was bending over her. Clustered about were the cast. Sally stood exactly where Nan had left her and Nan went quickly to her side.

"What happened?" she whispered.

"Miss Fair fainted just as the curtain fell. Oh, Nan, did you ever see anything like it? She must have a raging fever, but she played her part right up to the end."

"*Sssh!* She's coming to!"

Una Fair moaned and moved and quickly the doctor and a very worried looking Mr. Murray lifted her up between them and carried her off toward her dressing room.

A babel of conversation broke out immediately and Nan, followed closely by Sally, joined the group standing about in the center of the stage.

"I thought she was going to cave in before the curtain!" Hartley Bennett declared and mopped at his face, where perspiration was streaking his sideburns make-up.

"She'll never make it tomorrow," Mr. Hanig, who played the villain, asserted, "but she did a magnificent job."

"A real trouper," someone said.

As if to confirm these statements, Mr. Murray now walked out into the stage again.

"Where is Miss Graves?" he asked.

"I'm here." Helen stepped out from the wings.

"You will have to go on tomorrow. I want you to concentrate on *The Girl*. You can give your side for *Smilin'*

Through to Miss Van Delyss. Miss Van Delyss? Oh, there you are. You will take Miss Graves' place in the new play. All right, let's get out of here, all of you."

While they walked off-stage, Mr. Maguire's voice called, "Strike," and there was the noise of the shifting of scenery.

"I'm sorry you had to be here on such a night," Nan apologized to Sally, as they came out into the stage alley.

"I wouldn't have missed it for worlds! All my life I've heard about how the show must go on and now I've seen it! You've no idea how useless my sort of life seems beside this. I finished school two years ago. I'm twenty now and all I do is attend a round of parties with Mother, or perhaps take part in some affair for charity. I've begged and begged Mother to let me go to dramatic school and she's dead set against it. And I'm just as determined I will *not* go to college. It's not what I want at all. I'm not a bit of a brain. I'm going to try to see the show tomorrow again so I can watch that understudy. Is the box office still open, do you suppose?"

"No. But I'll pick up a ticket for you tomorrow, if you like. Let's see, could you come and have lunch with me and get it then?"

"I'll be here," Sally promised and then offered, "May I drive you home? I have my car."

So Nan was home much more quickly than usual. Sally, she thought, was a very nice girl and she felt sorry for her. Just imagine, at twenty, wanting something so much and still being unable to achieve it.

18

Nan's Good Deed

AT THE THEATER the following morning, there were all sorts
of rumors flying about concerning Miss Fair's condition.
There were those who were confident that she would be
able to finish out the week and those who were sure she
was all but dying.

It was Mr. Murray who finally gave the official word on
her illness.

"I regret to have to tell those of you who do not already
know it that Miss Fair has been hospitalized and will be
unlikely to return to us this season. As you know, she had
another week to play with us. In her place, for *Smilin'*
Through we are getting Lorna Dyke. She will fly
here tomorrow and will remain to do the other two shows
for which she is contracted. We are fortunate that she was
at liberty to come to us early. Miss Graves will finish out
the week in *The Girl*. We will have a quick reading of
Smilin' Through now and then I want a walk-through of
The Girl for Miss Graves at three o'clock.

The rehearsal began without delay. Even though the
part which was Una Fair's was being read by Peggy Worth,
Nan could tell that the play was one she would love. It
seemed to be the sort of play which was tender, gay and

sad by turns. Nan's part, her precious two lines, came in the first act. Though her throat felt dry as she heard the words of her cue, she managed to read her brief bit without faltering.

When the rehearsal was over, Nan went outside and found Sally already waiting for her.

"I'm sorry," Nan said, "but everything was at sixes and sevens this morning because Una Fair is in the hospital. Her part this week will be taken by Helen. I never got a chance to find out whether the box-office people were in. Come inside with me now and I'll see if I can find Mark. He'll know."

Mark, when found, said he thought he could locate the business manager and get the ticket, so the girls lingered near the bulletin board to wait for him.

They were still there when Mr. Murray came by. On a sudden impulse, Nan stopped him.

"Mr. Murray, may I speak to you a moment? This is a friend of mine, Sally Holly. Perhaps you know her mother, she was Marlene Price?"

"Of course, I remember her," Mr. Murray said, cordially holding out his hand. Sally looked dazed, as well she might, for she had no idea as to why Nan had introduced her to the director.

"Sally came backstage with me last night," Nan went on, "and she'd very much like to be able to watch some of the rehearsals. She is interested in the stage, but so far her mother won't consent to her going to a dramatic school, so I thought, maybe, if you'd let her watch—" Nan's voice trailed off as uncertainty about the enormity of her own boldness suddenly struck her. And at a time when Mr. Murray was so troubled, too!

His very preoccupation seemed to work in her favor, for

he answered hurriedly and a little absently, "Why certainly, yes, of course. Just so she's quiet. Glad to have met you. Tell your mother you look like her as I remember her."

Mr. Murray went on his way and Sally hugged her friend, whirling her about just as Mark came up to them.

"What happened?" he asked, then added, "I got you a seat—not a very good one, but a seat for tonight."

"Oh, you are dears and I love the lot of you!" Sally exclaimed and kissed the astonished Mark.

Nan giggled at his startled expression. "It's all right. She hasn't taken leave of her senses. It's just that Mr. Murray gave her permission to attend rehearsals any time she likes," she explained.

"That's swell!" Mark said.

"It was Nan who did it," Sally declared. "She stopped Mr. Murray and simply asked him if I might. I was never so surprised in my life. I had no idea what she was up to."

"To be frank with you, neither had I," Nan admitted. "It just came out—if I'd stopped to think about it, I guess I never would have said anything."

At this admission, Mark went off into a shout of laughter.

"Recommendation by Nan. Never *think!* If you do, you're sure not to speak! You are a pair of crazy girls! Well, come on, time's a'wasting, let's get something to eat."

At lunch, someone suggested that a collection be taken up for flowers to be sent to Miss Fair. Mark and Sally, as they were not involved in the walk-through, offered to take care of this. Nan, however, was too curious about the walk-through to join them. Theoretically she knew what the term meant, but she had never seen one.

A walk-through turned out to be just what its name implied. The action of the play was literally "walked-through" on the stage, with only a few lines spoken, to give the cues for the changing of positions and exits and entrances.

Nan was surprised at how calmly Helen took her assignment, but Bud Parks was impatient at her attitude. "I don't see why you think that to be an actress one has to go all fluttery. Sure, she's nervous, but she's had good training and she's a professional. She'll do her best and that's all."

It was, of course, the sensible attitude to take, Nan thought, and sighed. The real theater was so different from dramatic school. It asked hard work of you, expected you to play, even in illness, as Una Fair had, and gave you no time to yourself. It was hardhearted and practical on the one hand and shot through with sentiment on the other. Again Nan wondered if it was her world, though she loved it as she never had before.

At home, during supper, she told Mrs. Stockton about the day's happenings and about the arrangement she had brought about for Sally to watch the rehearsals.

"That was kind of you, Nan. I'm sure Sally will learn a great deal from it. I myself think she is cut out for the theater. She has always been a mimic, even as a small child. She has a lovely voice, speaking as well as singing, and it's the thing she has always wanted to do."

"Aunt Peggy," Nan said impulsively, "do you really think I belong in the theater, too?"

Mrs. Stockton paused before answering, as if she sensed the importance of a thoughtful reply.

"I was under the impression that you were *very sure* about what you wanted and completely absorbed in it. I do think you are adaptable and perhaps, if you have any doubts, it would be better for you to try some other way of life. This sort of question is so hard to answer for another person. What has made you question yourself?"

"Actually it has been a question in my mind all along. I *do* love the theater and I certainly try to do my best, but I've been afraid that perhaps mother's desire to have me an outstanding actress has influenced my choice. On the other hand, this summer I have begun to love the theater more and more and I'm never so happy as when I'm in it."

"Well, don't let it worry you, Nan. It is quite natural that your mother's choice for you would influence you. However, if it were entirely wrong for you, I doubt very much if you'd feel as you do now. At any rate, you've done your good deed for the day with Sally! Did it ever strike you how much easier it seems for youth to strongly desire what their parents are against? Take Sally, for instance. I suppose it is a form of growing up; to make your own choice, but if your choice and your mother's coincide, I don't think you should be upset by it."

Nan thought that over. "I guess you are right. I'd never thought of it just that way—but it is sort of 'fashionable' to want something your parents don't want!"

Mrs. Stockton smiled. "And you can't bear to be out of fashion, is that it?" They both laughed.

"Come now, Nan, it's almost time for you to be at the theater! This weekend you are going to go out to the club with us and play some tennis. You are looking pale."

"All right," Nan agreed readily, then smiled. Tennis, she thought, and flexed her right arm as she went into her room to pick up her purse. Tennis and the sun and easy laughter and perhaps a swim. How different people were! Sally and herself. Helen and Alicia. And Mark. Suddenly she wished Mark could come along to the club. Could have a real day off. He was sweet, but too serious, too intent.

19

Alicia Gives Advice

FOLLOWING THE SHOW that evening, the concensus of opinion was that Helen Graves had done a competent job as understudy—competent but uninspired.

She had added nothing new to the role. She had, in fact, deliberately aped Una Fair's every gesture. Yet Nan and many others felt that in her hands the role lacked vitality.

"Which should prove you wrong," Peggy Worth said to Bud one day when they were at Burt's without Helen. Peggy was referring, of course, to the old argument of *technical skill* versus *feeling*. As the argument raged to and fro, Nan kept silent. Not because she was entirely new and so ill at ease, as she had been before, but because for her the argument had a great personal meaning.

It was true that, once on the stage, she tended to "feel" the part, but beforehand, both in studying the part and in rehearsal, she remained aloof from it. She wondered if her feelings when on-stage were merely the result of excitement —of the lights and the indefinable but real tension that an audience communicated to the actors.

She wished desperately that she could talk out the whole matter with someone—not in the open give and take of wholesale discussion, but more intimately, with a friend and herself. She thought of Mark. But their hours always seemed to conflict. Nan wondered if Mark had noticed that he was not seeing as much of her as he had told her he hoped to. She knew she was disappointed and yet, contrary to Mark's predictions, it had been the theater which separated them and not the Stocktons.

The discussion had reached one of those impasses that all such discussions reach. Neither Bud nor Peggy would give an inch and the matter was dropped as they all left the restaurant.

Alicia and Nan were walking when the former burst out suddenly, "Well, thank goodness, this week is almost over! If I had to watch that 'Grave' girl another week, I'd be in my grave!"

"Oh, Alicia, surely she's not as bad as all that! Actually she follows Una Fair's interpretation pretty closely," Nan protested.

Alicia grunted. "That's the whole trouble! She has tried to make a carbon copy and, like a carbon, it is not clearly defined. I wish I'd had her chance!"

"You've said that before. Suppose you had—what would you have done differently?" Nan challenged her.

"Look—do you know any of the lines by heart?"

Nan thought and realized that she did carry in her mind whole sections of the play. It surprised her and her surprise showed in her voice, "Why, yes—I guess I do!"

"O.K. Then come on down to the hotel room with me and I'll show you what I mean. I'm just a little sick of having everyone think I'm merely bragging when I say I can do a part. I *know* I can."

Nan hesitated a moment and then replied, "All right—I'll go with you, but I'll have to phone home first and tell Aunt

Peggy I'll be eating out. I couldn't get back for the performance otherwise."

Nan made her call and, if Mrs. Stockton was surprised to hear that Nan and Alicia were together, she did not say so, merely suggesting that Nan come straight home from the theater that night, if she was to play tennis the following day.

In Alicia's room, the two girls placed chairs and tables in positions similar to those on stage and took a scene between the leading woman and the villain to work on.

Even knowing, as she did, what Alicia was capable of, Nan was startled at the new interpretation she gave to Miss Fair's lines.

When they were finished, Nan sat down on the edge of the bed and said, "It was wonderful, Alicia. How did you ever think of a different way from Miss Fair's?"

Alicia shrugged, and the hard tone in which she answered grated on Nan's ears.

"Because there are *always* different ways of doing any part. There are no stereotypes. Miss Fair played the part breezily and a little stridently—and it's good that way. But the woman herself could just as easily be langorous and a little hard. That's how I'd make her come alive."

"Alicia," Nan said suddenly, "There has been a lot of talk, like today at Burt's, about *feeling* a part, or being *technically proficient* at it. It troubles me. You see, I'm not at all sure of myself. Not the way you are. You do 'feel' a part, don't you?"

"If you mean by 'feel' that I feel tragic or gay or sad with the character; no. I think that way lies amateurishness and it almost never gets across to an audience. But to steep yourself in the character *first*, to 'feel' deep down how that person might act and then apply your technique and make it seem as though you *are* that person—that is acting."

"You are conscious then that you are acting?"

"Yes, always."

"It makes sense. I guess my trouble is I tend to skip the preparation end. You know I've only got that bit part in the next play, but I suppose even that person should seem real to me?"

"Certainly. What kind of a life does she lead? Is she at the wedding party with the boy she loves? Or is she there just for a good time? Or is she bored? Think it out."

"Gee, Alicia it—it makes the whole play more exciting! I never tried to build up a life for a character outside the limits of the script. I wonder why I never thought of it."

"Perhaps because you don't want the stage as much as I do," Alicia said, and for the first time Nan heard complete sincerity in the older girl's voice.

What a strange person she is, Nan thought. If she could only play a part calling for a bit more humility in her own life—and warmth—she'd be a likable person. Aloud she said, "I'm ever so grateful, Alicia, really I am. And I'll certainly back up any claims you make after this."

Nan meant it wholeheartedly, but Alicia replied wryly, "That's nice of you, my pet. But you really don't have much influence, after all, do you?"

Nan felt as if she had been slapped. To cover her hurt, she said hastily, "We'd better get something to eat, hadn't we? It's getting late."

Alicia glanced at her watch and exclaimed, "Goodness— it's time I was downstairs! I've a dinner date. I suppose you can get something to eat here—or at the cafeteria down the street."

"I'll go to the cafeteria," Nan told her. "I'm sorry if I made you late."

"Oh, it'll do him good to wait. It never hurts a man to wait. 'Bye, be seeing you," and Alicia shut the door firmly after Nan.

Nan was furious, and yet, with her usual striving for fairness, she reflected as she ate her lonely supper that Alicia had *not* asked her to dinner. And she had obtained something of value from her, hateful and hurtful though she could be.

As she took the bus back to the theater, Nan smiled wryly to herself. Here was a character ripe for interpretation. What manner of girl was Alicia? What made her tick? How could she be so good an actress and so shoddy a person?

20

Advice Put in Practice

THE OPENING SCENE of the forthcoming production of *Smilin' Through* was in a garden, which a group of young people were decorating with Japanese lanterns in preparation for a wedding party. The action which was to take place was simple.

One of the boys (Bud Parks had the part) climbed up on a bench to hang a lantern, which Nan was to hand to him. At this point he was to act as though he had lost his balance and was about to fall. Immediately, the boys and girls were to shriek and run toward him, presenting a pretty composition of hoop-skirted figures, for it was a costume play.

In the previous rehearsals, Mr. Murray had asked them to repeat the small scene several times.

"Put more life into it!" he had begged them. "This is a gay scene and it sets itself in contrast to the tragedy that is about to take place. You are all young, lively, eager—pick it up! Pick it up!"

Try as they would, however, the scene would not come alive. Nan knew this and today she, for one, meant to really try.

Thinking over Alicia's advice, she had created for herself

a character to fit the girl she was playing. The girl was, she had decided, younger than the rest and it was her first "grown-up" party. She was eager, even over-anxious, to be of help. She then would be the one to really cry out when the boy began to fall, because she was more keyed up than the rest.

Nan hoped she would be able to put across the feeling she had in mind and she was glad it was the first day that they were to be on-stage. It seemed easier, somehow, to act with abandon on a stage, rather than in the more confined area of the greenroom.

When the scene began, Nan put all the sparkle she could into her face and voice. So far it seemed to be good, but there was a little cloud of doubt in her mind as to how convincingly she could scream, when the moment came.

It was about time now— She reached up with the lantern to hand it to the boy and then it happened! The bench on which Bud stood tipped perilously. He was, in actual fact, about to fall. Nan screamed—a wholly realistic scream. Like an echo of herself, the others screamed too and rushed toward them. The bench righted itself and Mr. Murray's voice came out of the darkness in front.

"Stop! That's good. That's more like it! Nan Lane, that's what I've been trying to get you to do. Now, try it again."

They played it over and, though the bench did not actually tip this time, Nan was able to reproduce her scream. It was as if it had been recorded in her vocal cords, just as it had been wrung from her before.

The play went on. Nan's brief part was over. Off-stage, she found that her knees were weak, her throat dry and her heart pounding rapidly. Yet, despite these reactions, her heart sang. She had done it! She had pleased the director and into a two-line part she had brought life. This was acting!

Quietly now, she watched the rest of the rehearsal. When it was over, Mark came up to her.

"Good girl!" he said.

"Thanks! I'll tell you a secret, though, Mark. The first time we played the scene, Bud actually came near to falling. I don't think Mr. Murray noticed though, from out front. *That* scream was for real and the nice part of it is that I was able to do it again so it sounded just the same. I think I begin to see a bit of what Alicia told me. She said, the other day, that for her (and I believe now for me) the most important part of learning a role was to conceive the character first in your mind as a real person. From this conception you build up the reality of the part, and even direction can only modify it, not change it, if it is well thought out. Don't you think that's good?"

Mark pulled thoughtfully at the lobe of his ear. He had been listening with close interest. "Yes, I do," he agreed. "When did she talk to you about this? I didn't think you saw much of her."

Nan shrugged. "I don't actually. But I was troubled— I have been right along—about something lacking in myself. So I asked her, on impulse, what made her so sure of herself where acting was concerned. The whole thing started because she'd criticized Helen's work. Well, Alicia took me to her room and we went over bits of *The Girl*. Mark she gave the lead a totally different interpretation from Una Fair's. It was *good*—not necessarily better than Miss Fair's, but lots better than Helen's copy of Una Fair. Then she explained to me how she 'thought out' even the smallest part. So I tried to do that today and it worked! Oh, I realize the scream was torn from me—but even without it, I think I did the part better."

They had been walking upstairs slowly as they talked and now they stopped in front of Nan's dressing room.

"So that is the story of my great success, sir," Nan concluded lightly. It was on the tip of her tongue to tell him about how let down she had felt by the rest of Alicia's behavior, but something held her back.

Alicia had been kind enough to help her by really discussing her problem and it was not a nice thing to belittle that kindness by reporting her well-known faults all over again. So Nan kept still—and was glad later on that she had.

21

Jealousy

AFTER THE PLAY WAS OVER on Saturday night, Nan found Mark waiting for her.

"Want to go for a cup of coffee?" he asked.

"Mark, I can't. I promised Aunt Peggy I'd come straight home after the show."

"How about tomorrow? A movie, maybe?"

"Oh, Mark! I do wish you'd asked me before. I promised Aunt Peggy I'd play tennis tomorrow. She thinks I'm looking pale."

"You don't look a bit pale to me; but go along and enjoy yourself. I'll find something to do. 'Bye, see you Monday."

" 'Bye Mark," Nan said in a small voice, and the tears came to her eyes as she watched his retreating back. He'd not even offered to take her to the bus. She wished she had thought to say "give me a rain check" or some such thing, but, as usual, she had just been dumb!

On the way to the bus, Nan saw Sally's parked car and thought, "My goodness, do you suppose she saw the show again?" There was no one near it, however, and her own thoughts occupied her so that she did not give Sally another thought.

At home, she told the Stocktons a bit about her conversation at the hotel and what it had led to for her that day.

She admitted her debt to Alicia. "I do wish I understood her, though," she declared.

"If I were you, I'd get to bed and not lose any sleep worrying over understanding Alicia," Mrs. Stockton advised when she saw Nan trying to suppress a yawn.

"I won't lose sleep over anyone," Nan assured her. "I'm dead tired."

"I've been thinking, Nan, I should have asked you to bring one of your own friends along for tennis. Perhaps Mark? I do wish you'd ask anyone you wish, of your own accord. You know we will welcome them any time."

"You are so awfully good to me. I—I never would have asked anyone just all by myself, though I did sort of wish Mark could have a day in the sun, too. He asked me to go to the movies with him, matter of fact; but I'm dying to be outdoors and you asked me first, of course, so I said no."

"Oh, Nan, I don't want you to turn down dates for me! On the other hand, I do think a day in the sun would be good for you. I wish you had asked the boy to come along, why didn't you?"

"I just never thought of it—I mean I don't belong to the club, I'm a guest there myself and well, it just never occurred to me!"

"Nan, will you get it into your head that your friends are welcome here, or at the club, any time you want them?"

"I didn't know about the club. Thank you, Aunt Peggy. Maybe another Sunday we could take Mark?"

"Of course, dear. Now run along."

Nan went gladly and was asleep almost as soon as she lay down.

It was almost noon the next day when Nan and the Stocktons started for the club. Nan was carrying the racket she had chosen from several in the hall closet. The day was perfect and not too hot, for a change, and Nan felt good. It would be fun to play tennis again!

When they reached the club, she did not immediately see anyone she knew, but soon Mary Riner came out of the clubhouse.

"Hello, Nan. Going to play tennis?" Mary asked.

"I'd hoped to, but I don't see anyone I know just now."

"I was trying to find someone for doubles," Mary said, smiling, "so consider yourself that someone. I'll get my racket and collect the other two and be with you in a sec'."

"Do I know the others?" Nan asked.

"Jud and Roger," Mary answered.

"Jud? By himself? Where's Sally?"

"Hasn't put in an appearance yet and Jud's sore. Called her house and she'd left."

"Did they have a date?"

"They never have a date—they're just always together. Jud's so mad right now he will probably lick us all single-handed."

Presently Mary and the two young men came out, rackets in hand. Roger was quietly courteous, as always, and Jud acknowledged Nan's presence with a half-muttered "Hello" and went right on scowling.

Oh, dear! Nan thought. I hope I don't get him for a partner.

But she did, And it worked out well. Mary and Nan were only fair players. Roger was very good—better than Jud, ordinarily, Nan suspected. But today was not ordinary and all Jud's frustration was vented in playing a hard, driving game.

They were tied at the end of the first set and, after the deciding game was played, with Jud and Nan taking the set, Nan was glad enough to stretch out on the grass and let the sun soak into her.

"How's the work?" Roger asked.

"Fine. I've a two-line part next week," Nan announced proudly.

"I wish you'd never taken Sally with you," Jud said abruptly. "Oh, I know you thought it was a nice thing to do, but all I hear now is the theater. What Mr. Murray said —how Una Fair feels—what Miss Graves did or didn't do. What Mr. Bennett said—and Mark, Mark, Mark!"

"Mark!" exclaimed Nan.

"Yes, Mark. Why? Friend of yours?"

"Yes he is. A good friend."

"Well, Sally quotes him all the time. Seems he's been helping her to digest all the rehearsals she's seen."

Nan remained silent, troubled. She had not known that Sally and Mark were seeing each other, not having seen much of them herself during the past week.

Suddenly Jud sat upright. "There's Sally's car now. Wonder whatever kept her—had me worried. She's a crazy driver."

Why Jud really loves her, Nan thought. He was worried, not angry.

All four of them watched the car as it turned into the parking lot, but at least two of them were not prepared for what happened then. Out of the car stepped Sally and, with her, Mark emerged.

"Who on earth is that?" Jud asked.

"That," said Nan, and was surprised when her voice shook, "that is Mark."

Sally and Mark had seen the quartette of tennis players and, apparently unaware of all the stir they'd caused waved gaily and came walking toward them.

Sally introduced Mark and, after he'd greeted them, he, and Sally too, sat down on the grass.

"I phoned and you'd left," Jud said accusingly.

Sally seemed unconcerned. She answered in a matter of fact way, "Yes, I didn't have time to call you first because I promised last night to pick up Mark and I overslept. Played a set?"

"Yes."

"*Mmm*. Well, Mark and I came for a swim. You going to play some more, or do you want to go to the pool?"

"I'd like a swim," Nan answered quickly.

"Good! Let's all go then. Oh, by the way, Nan, did you know Miss Fair's husband came for her today and she has left the hospital and is on her way home?"

"I'm glad. I didn't know she *had* a husband, though."

"Oh, yes. Most actresses keep their own names when they get married."

Jud snorted. "Lot of nonsense," he declared. "I'd like to see any wife of mine going around as Miss Somebody-or-other."

For the first time in a long while Nan heard the old sarcastic Sally. "No Miss Somebody-or-other, nor any Miss Nobody-or-other, for that matter, has accepted your offer of marriage as yet," she flared, and, turning to Mark, she tucked his hand possessively under her arm. "Let's go. I want you to show me that crawl stroke you told me won the cup for you."

Following more slowly, with the amiable Roger, the quiet Mary and the furiously silent Jud, Nan hoped that Sally hadn't decided to really go all out for Mark. Sally was too attractive a girl and apparently Mark had quite easily overcome his feeling against wealth, at least where Sally was concerned.

Why, oh why, didn't I go to the movies with him—or ask him here? Nan thought. Evidently he had opened up to Sally or how would she know anything about a cup he had won for swimming? By the time the six young people were dressed for the pool, Nan was in almost as black a mood as Jud.

Nor was her mood improved during the remainder of the day.

Not only was Mark an excellent swimmer, but when dinner time came, Nan found that Mark was also an exceptionally good dancer.

"What's bothering you, Nan?" he asked as he dipped and turned during their second dance together.

"Why nothing at all—what would be?" Nan answered, struggling to keep her voice lightly amused.

"You seem very quiet," Mark insisted.

"I'm not the loud type, at least I never thought I was."

"I didn't say that. But between you and Jud, this might be a morticians' ball."

"I just find the evening a bit dull," Nan admitted.

Mark went into a series of fancy steps that required all Nan's concentration to follow before he answered, "That's odd. I'm enjoying myself. It *is* better than the movies. No wonder you turned me down for Jud."

"Mark, I never did! I—" but the end of her sentence was lost in the patter of applause as the dance ended and Mark escorted her back to their table.

Nor did she dance with him again.

At the table, Mark talked golf knowingly with Mr. Stockton, flirted outrageously with Sally and, in general, behaved as Nan would never have thought he could behave.

It did not soothe her ruffled feelings to be told in the car on the way home how *very* nice Mrs. Stockton thought Mark was.

"A really brilliant boy. So good looking, too. He was so quiet and shy the first time you brought him home that I really didn't see what you saw in him particularly. I'm afraid he has upset Jud considerably. But it won't hurt that young man a bit—he's far too conceited for his own good and he's so sure of Sally—or was."

Nan made no attempt to answer, but murmured that she'd better get to bed and get some rest because tomorrow would be a tough day.

Once in bed, however, she lay staring into the darkness. It was all right to say it didn't hurt Jud to see Sally with Mark, but what about her? She wasn't conceited—or was she?

She began to realize that she'd taken Mark pretty much for granted, too. She'd placed him as an attentive, hard working boy to whom she felt attracted. A boy who had already all but told her she was the one he cared for and now he was—he was, another Alicia! With that thought, Nan's long withheld tears fell.

There wasn't a more miserable nor homesick girl anywhere that night than Nan Lane.

22

Blowup

NAN WAKENED feeling heavy-eyed and cross. It was already hot and she had a real temptation to stay home and rest. Today was a first reading, though, and she knew she had no chance at a part unless she showed up.

Rather perfunctorily, she knelt to say her morning prayers. As had often happened before, the act of prayer started a chain of thought. Nan rose from her knees, sat on the edge of bed and took stock of herself. What she found she did not like. True, she had been hurt yesterday, or had thought she was, but actually it was she who, being previously committed, had turned down two invitations from Mark. Could she blame him then if he had accepted Sally's invitation?

Her disappointment had stemmed from a spirit of poor sportsmanship of which she was suddenly ashamed. Instead of being glad that Mark had fitted in so well with the Country Club crowd, she had been upset. Why? Because she had appropriated Mark to herself. If she had brought him to the club and he had behaved exactly as he had, she would have been proud!

And what of her work? Was she trying as hard as she had promised herself she would? So far, of course, she had not had any great opportunities to do more than observe.

Still, even this passive work might have been more fruitful, she felt.

I'll do better and try not to be jealous, or mean, to anyone, she thought.

Feeling much better after her session of self-criticism, Nan bathed, dressed and went her way.

Before the cast assembled she had a chance to speak to Mark and, obeying her own promise to herself, she said, "I'm glad Sally took you out to the club. I'd have liked to have done that myself, but, after all, I didn't know if I could, since I was a guest myself. Matter of fact I asked Mrs. Stockton on Saturday night if I could invite you and she said I might. So, will you go with me next week?"

Mark's mobile face lighted with pleasure. "Sure, I will," he answered. "I enjoyed it all a lot, but I think it burned Jud up that I was there with Sally. And I'd rather be with you, anyway."

"Thanks," Nan flushed, then added, "You're right; Jud was furious."

"There's nothing between Sally and myself but friendship," Mark asserted. "She wants so badly to go on the stage and she asks me all sorts of questions about the rehearsals. I don't know half as much as she gives me credit for."

"You know a lot, Mark. You know a lot of other things, too, I'm beginning to discover. Where did you learn to swim so well? You never told me about winning cups and all that!"

"Oh, that! I belonged to a CYO team while I was in school and I took some cups and medals. I learned about golf from being a caddie. I even got started in the theater through our CYO plays."

"You've always made the most of all your chances, haven't you? You never just drifted into something because someone else wanted you to?"

Mark smiled. "Worrying about yourself?"

Nan nodded unhappily.

"Perhaps it's being a part of a large family does it, Nan. I can't explain it, except that, much as my parents love me, they aren't *absorbed* in me. They can't be. There have been times when I wished they were; but I begin to think that maybe it is easier to develop your own capacities when you have to depend on yourself more."

"I'm sure you're right. Anyway, I'm really going to buckle down now. I do like the theater—more and more, I think—but I've let a lot of side interests pull me here and there. Then too, I've been afraid to admit the fact that I really may like the theater myself—that if I do, it's not just my mother's choice for me, but my own."

They didn't have a chance to talk further before rehearsal began, but Nan felt infinitely better. How humble Mark was—and how honest!

When Sally came in and quietly took her place, Nan was able to smile at her wholeheartedly.

It was mid-week before the rehearsals moved on-stage and, for the first time since she had come to the company, Nan saw Mr. Murray throw the sort of temperamental fit directors were reputed to be prone to.

The new star, Lorna Dyke, was younger than Una Fair and not nearly so assured. In the current play, she tended to overplay her role, despite constant pressure from the director to tone down her performance.

On Thursday he suddenly shouted at her from the darkness of the orchestra pit, where he had been pacing back and forth, "Stop! Stop it, I say! I've told you over and over how I want that line said. Quietly—not as if you were declaiming in a high school play." Rapidly Mr. Murray strode onto the stage and, taking Lorna Dyke by the shoulders, he fairly pushed her off into the wings.

"Now, give me the cue," he said to Mr. Hanig, who was on-stage.

Obediently, Mr. Hanig repeated his cue line.

Nan had a difficult time not to giggle. It seemed so funny to see Mr. Murray, shirt-sleeved, hot and angry, play Lorna Dyke's part; yet she realized that, despite his male voice and appearance, he did give the lines a more casual tone.

"There now, take it over—" he said when he had finished.

Once more they began and once more he stopped them—again and once again until Lorna Dyke burst into tears.

"O.K.! O.K.! We'll call it a day. But for Pete's sake *think*. *Think* of the part. Go home and soak in it. I want it played the way I directed it and *no other way*, by to-morrow."

No one said a word while they all filed out, but Nan saw Mr. Hanig pat Miss Dyke's shoulder consolingly as they walked along.

"Whew!" Sally exclaimed, coming up to Nan, "I'm glad I'm just observing. Though he's right, of course."

Mark strolled over to them. "Go for coffee?" he asked.

"Sure thing. I have to wait around for Jud. He said he'd call for me about one."

"He was awfully upset yesterday, wasn't he?" Mark asked.

Sally admitted it and added in almost precisely Mrs. Stockton's words of the night before, "Not that it will hurt him. He's spoiled and far too sure of me."

"Don't you want him to be sure?" Mark asked gently.

Sally faltered a moment before she answered. "Well, yes, I suppose I do, really. I'm awfully fond of Jud and we've always dated. But he hates my even thinking about the theater. There he and my mother agree."

"Would your thinking of the theater, as you put it, mean that you would have to put him out of your life?"

"Oh, no! I never thought of that!" Sally protested.

"Can't you make him see that?"

Nan sat silent as the two of them discussed Sally's problem over their coffee. Her own mind wandered to the scene between the director and Lorna Dyke and she came to with a start when Sally addressed her directly. "Nan, you wouldn't mind if I dated Mark, now and again, would you? I think it might teach Jud a lesson."

Swallowing her dismay, Nan answered as steadily as she could, "That's up to Mark. Though I'm not at all sure that making anyone miserable and jealous is the right way."

"Nor am I," Mark agreed. "However, you'll see him soon, Sally, and perhaps it'll straighten itself out. Anyway, Nan and I have a week-end date, so for this week you'll have to pick on someone else."

Sally smiled and shrugged as they all rose, having finished their coffee, and strolled outside, where they were confronted by the sight of Jud in earnest, even eager, conversation with Alicia.

"Oh, oh!" Mark exclaimed. "I'm afraid your friend has the same idea."

Ruefully, Sally agreed and then said with energy, "Well, I don't intend to let either Jud or the stage go, not without a fight."

"Good girl, that's the spirit," Mark said softly as they crossed the street and made their way to Jud's car.

23

Jud Threatens

To EVERYONE'S RELIEF, Lorna Dyke's performance the next day came close enough to Mr. Murray's directions so that a further scene was averted and the rehearsal went smoothly.

Nan saw little of Mark, except at luncheon with all the rest, during the week.

Her Sunday date with him at the club was pleasant and uneventful. Neither Sally nor Jud were there that day and it was more peaceful without their feuding.

Nan and Mark played doubles with Mary Riner and Roger, who as usual, seemed unattached. Afterwards they swam and then sat down to a bridge game, suggested by Roger, but Nan was a careless player and Mark an uncertain one, so presently the talk drifted to the theater.

Roger told them some of the ideas he had for plays and, to Nan's surprise, Mark spoke of his dream of a children's theater. Roger seemed very interested and mostly the young men talked, while Nan and Mary listened.

Mary did ask if Jud and Sally had been quarreling, but as no one seemed to know, the matter was not pursued.

Nan and Mark joined the Stocktons for dinner and shortly afterward they drove Mark home to his boarding house. Nan was so tired she almost fell asleep in the car and apologized to Mark, as he left, for her dullness.

He laughed. "That's all right. I'm glad you weren't any ball of fire! I'm pretty tired myself. I've really enjoyed the day enormously though," he turned to his hosts, "and I do thank you. I bet I'll sleep tonight!"

"Me, too!" Nan agreed . . . and yawned.

On this prosaic, but oddly companionable note, they parted and when she reached home Nan did indeed sleep well.

The following week was also uneventful, except that Peggy Worth had started a series of readings from classical plays which they all attended, whenever they could, and which Nan thoroughly enjoyed.

On Monday morning, Nan expected that a new play would be cast, as usual. Ever since Una Fair's illness, Mr. Murray had cast regular understudies for the leading parts. He had also recommended that all the extra members of the cast and the students be prepared with a working knowledge of the play, so that, in case of necessity, they would be able to take any part for which they were needed. This practice had quickened Nan's interest in the rehearsals.

She had been consistently following Alicia's advice, given at the hotel that evening not so long ago, and was often able to invest a small "bit" part with a feeling of reality. So Monday mornings held for her an element of suspense. Would she be fortunate enough to understudy the lead? Would there be a bit part for her? If not, was there a part that especially interested her and that, on her own, she could develop?

Nan was so concerned with these thoughts that she had

almost turned into the alley leading to the stage door before she heard her name called repeatedly.

"Nan! Nan!"

She stopped and looked about, puzzled. Then she saw Jud. He was standing at the corner of the theater. Obviously he had been peeking out toward the alley until he saw her come along.

Reluctantly, not wishing to be involved, yet unable to pretend she'd not seen him, Nan went over to him.

"Hello, Jud, what brings you here so early?" She attempted to make her question sound casual.

"Come around to the front of the building and I'll tell you," he said, taking her hand and pulling her after him. He glanced down the street both ways and then, seeing no one, relaxed back against the building.

"Was Sally out at the club with Mark yesterday?" he demanded.

Startled at the question, as she had been there with Mark herself, Nan answered, "She wasn't there at all."

An angry frown creased Jud's brow. "If I get my hands on that guy—" he began.

"Don't be stupid," Nan broke in sharply. "Mark *was* at the club—with me. I don't know where Sally was."

"You needn't try to protect him! Sally's so mad for the theater she'd take up with anyone. He's nothing but a cheap fortune hunter. He could never give her what she wants and is used to."

It was on the tip of Nan's tongue to tell Jud that she was not lying and that he could easily verify Mark's presence at the club with her by speaking to Roger or Mary Riner. Instead, she retorted angrily, "You're acting like a small boy, Jud. Certainly Sally loves the theater and you and her mother are driving her more and more toward it by your opposition. As to Mark, I guess he can take care of himself—and besides, I know him pretty well and I don't think he's really interested in Sally."

Jud hesitated and seemed on the brink of believing her, but he suddenly scowled again.

"Then tell him to keep away from her, because I am interested in her," he ordered.

Nan saw that he would not listen to reason and, feeling impatient with his moods, she said curtly, "Well, I can't help you. I can see that. Besides, I'll be late for rehearsal." And, turning her back on him, she left.

On entering the greenroom, Nan saw in a glance that both Mark and Sally were already present, as were most of the others, but before she could speak to them the roll call began.

Mr. Murray announced that their new play was to be *Seventh Heaven*.

To Nan's intense delight and excitement, she was assigned to understudy the lead.

After the reading broke up for lunch period, several members of the cast congratulated her and Nan had almost forgotten her encounter with Jud when Sally came up to add her congratulations.

"Look, Sally, I have something to see you about, privately, before lunch. Come into the theater with me for a moment," Nan urged.

Puzzled, Sally followed her into the dimness of the orchestra seats. There Nan told her about her conversation with Jud.

"The funny part of it is," Sally remarked, when Nan had finished, "that I wasn't out with anyone but my mother. I told her the time had come when I simply had to settle this business about the theater with her, once and for all.

Knowing that one or the other of us would likely be called on a Sunday, we took a long drive and didn't leave any word, except that we would be gone for the day."

"Did you settle the question with your mother?"

"Yes. Oh, Nan she has relented and she's going to let me go to dramatic school this fall, and she says I can go right on attending rehearsals here this summer."

"I *am* glad! But what about Jud?"

"Jud will have to accept it, that's all. I do care for him, Nan, but he has to learn not to be so possessive. A year apart will be good for both of us. Meanwhile, I shall do as I please."

"But what about Mark? Jud did threaten."

"Poof! He won't really do anything—especially if I don't continue to date Mark. That was my mistake in the beginning. You're fond of Mark, aren't you?"

"Yes. Yes, I am. Though we've never really said anything serious about ourselves. I never seem to see him any more for one thing." Again Nan was aware of how much she wished she could see more of Mark.

"He's nice. I wish you luck. Look, if we don't get lunch now, we won't get any. Let's go."

Together the girls left the building to go to Burt's. There was no sign of Jud and Mark was already eating. They joined him, relieved, and talked theater.

24

Nan Gives Advice

NAN BEGAN THE LEARNING of her part as understudy in earnest that same day. Excusing herself to the Stocktons, she closeted herself in her room and read the part over and over until her eyes began to close with fatigue.

When at last she had finished, had a hot bath and climbed into bed, she was able to repeat a large part of the role to herself. It was, she decided, easy to memorize.

It was a little discouraging then to find, on waking the next morning, that there were large gaps in her memory of the lines. Nan knew very well that it was unlikely she would get a chance to play the part, but because she wanted to (it was a lovely part), she could not rest content until she had learned her lines thoroughly.

She propped the script in front of her at the breakfast table, explaining to Annie its great importance. Usually, with Mrs. Stockton still abed, and Mr. Stockton already at the office, Nan and Annie chatted amiably over Nan's breakfast.

"I'm that glad for you now!" Annie really sounded pleased. "I wish the leadin' lady no misfortune, mind you, but a wee bit of a cold, maybe?"

Nan laughed. "Oh, Annie! Still, do you know, I believe

I'd be scared to death if I really had the chance to go on handed to me."

"I don't believe it! Now then, get to your studyin', but mind you eat some breakfast, too. You'll need it!"

"I will, Annie, I promise," Nan answered, and kept her word, though if she had been asked afterwards what she ate, it was doubtful that she could have remembered.

The play, *Seventh Heaven*, as it developed at the rehearsals, was a touching romance of the Paris Latin Quarter. Miss Dyke was far better suited for her part in it than for the parts she had played before.

"Which just goes to show you she's not much of an actress, when casting her to type makes a difference," Alicia the ever critical said.

"I think I'd feel more secure if she wasn't so *well* cast this time," Nan confessed.

"Why?"

"Well—just in case I did have to go on for her, the contrast wouldn't be so obvious."

"Are you doing badly?"

"I don't really know. Oh, I know all the lines, but it's hard to tell, by yourself."

"Tell you what—I'll cue you this afternoon, if you like, and we can eat together afterwards. I don't have a date this time," Alicia said frankly.

"That would be swell. Only why not come to the house with me? Aunt Peggy says I may bring anyone I wish, at any time. Do come!"

"O.K. After the matinee, then." It was a mid-week matinee day and Alicia had a part in the current play.

Nan had time to wonder, before she met Alicia at the bus stop that afternoon, whether she had again made a mistake in inviting her. However, she could see nothing in Alicia's offer to cue her save one of her unaccountable streaks of friendliness. Knowing the girl, though, she was cautious about the whole affair, waiting for an ulterior motive to show, like a tattered petticoat, beneath the smooth surface.

Alicia commented favorably on the Stockton place, showed suitable interest in some "snaps" that Nan had just received from home and then they went to work.

Working with Alicia was like being coached by a real director. As usual, she had grasped the characters of the play and made them her own—a few times over for the more difficult scenes, an explanation here or there, or per- haps a bit of technique.

"Look, pet, if you'll turn your head there—when Chico says that—just there, so. Lift your head and then, holding it still half-turned from the audience, swallow, then let your head droop slowly. Try it—there—nice effect."

Nan could feel that it was. When they had finished she said gratefully, "Really, Alicia, I don't know how I can thank you enough. I feel so—so much more confident now. Why, if Lorna Dyke were stricken, I honestly believe I could take over!"

"Of course you could. I hope you'll get the chance. It would be fine for you if Lorna Dyke got sick."

"You don't really mean that, do you, Alicia?"

"Of course I do! Why not? It is what understudies pray for and, don't forget, Miss Dyke isn't so far from her own beginnings, when she wished disaster on the star. You are such an innocent, how did you ever turn up in this business?"

Nan flushed and then said, in self-defense, what she had often wished to say and never quite dared, "Alicia I don't know whether you believe all you say, but I do think, sincerely, that you are wrong. I've found that the bigger a person is, the less hard they are. It's people like Miss Trevor, Una Fair, Mr. Murray—yes, and the Stocktons, too, who are unfailingly helpful to beginners."

"Naturally, they can afford to be. They've already arrived."

"No, you're wrong. I can't prove it, of course, because I didn't know them before they arrived, but I believe they always had that quality of being less self-centered and self-ish to begin with. Perhaps they didn't have as much initial talent as some one else, but they were willing to work and they were—outgoing to others. I don't mean that the hard ones don't get along, too—it would be naive to believe that —but I do think they make it harder for themselves. They stand in their own way."

"You think then that I do myself harm—with all my talent—by my attitude?"

Subtly the conversation had changed its emphasis from a discussion of generalities to Alicia personally. But Nan stuck to her point fearlessly. "Yes, I do. You are quite right about your talent. Everyone recognizes it, but it shouldn't make you so intolerant of others. You're not even friendly most of the time. You have been to me, I'll admit, and you've helped me before. But then you'd cut me just as quickly if it served your purpose, or mood, wouldn't you?"

"I don't have any false loyalties, that's all."

"But, don't you see, Alicia, it's not loyalty to *me* or to anyone else you need. It's loyalty to yourself. To the best in you. I—I can't explain it very well—" Nan ended lamely.

Alicia smiled. "You go your way and I'll go mine," she said lightly.

Nan stammered, "I—I'm sorry. I shouldn't have said all that—and just when I'm so grateful to you, too."

Whether the strange conversation would have continued or not, Nan did not find out, for Mrs. Stockton came to the door to say that dinner was ready and to greet Alicia.

The two girls did not mention their talk again, though Nan felt a sense of embarrassment every time she thought of it. Still, she was curiously glad she had spoken out.

25

Repayment

SEVENTH HEAVEN played to packed houses and, for the first time that season, it was decided to hold a play over for a second week.

Mr. Murray beamed upon his cast on Monday of the second week.

"You've all done a good job this season, so I'm going to give you a break. We will not hold any more rehearsals of *Peter Ibbetson* until Thursday. Three days' holiday. But I want no sunburn cases, no fatigue, no hangovers on Thursday. Have a good time."

A babble of conversation broke out as each one, from the stars to the students, welcomed the news.

"I'm just going to sleep and sleep—" someone said.

"Me for some golf," Mr. Hanig declared.

"I'll settle for a cool spot and a book." That was Bud.

As Nan, Mark, Helen, Bud, Sally and Peggy Worth left the theater together, Nan saw Alicia turn down the side street, alone as usual. Sally followed Nan's glance and said bitterly, "I'm glad to see the last of her for a while."

"She's not bad when you get to know her," Nan protested.

"I don't want to know her any better than I do. Jud can

do that for me." Sally's voice shook with anger. "Do you know he had the nerve to tell me that, if I had her talent, he wouldn't mind my going on the stage! He wouldn't recognize talent if he fell over it."

"But she is talented. You know yourself how well she has been doing as a stand-in for the lead in *Peter Ibbetson*. Everyone says she's marvelous. I even heard that maybe there won't be a visiting star and Mr. Murray will use her when we produce the play. He hasn't said who she is standing in for, you know."

"Oh, I know it. Of course, I know it. And do you think it makes it any easier for me? I can't even get a chance to show what I might do—not even to prove a point to Jud— while she— Oh, skip it!"

Nan changed the subject gladly. "Are you going out to the club?"

"I don't know," Sally answered shortly.

Nan was sorry for her but, in her present mood, there was no use trying to talk to her. Dear me, Nan thought, what a cross-grained love affair can do! Ordinarily, Sally was a sweet girl, especially here at the theater.

After coffee at Burt's, Peggy Worth invited Nan, Helen and Sally to her room at the hotel. Nan accepted, as did Helen, but while Sally was hesitating, Mark said, "Sally, I have to bring back that garden chair and table we used as props in the last show. If you have your car, would you drive me out to the club with them?"

"Love to," Sally said, brightening.

Bud Parks shrugged in mock dejection. "Leaves poor Buddy boy all by himself," he moaned. But none of them felt really sorry for him. He was used to being alone and, even when in the theater, often carried a book with him and read at odd moments. Now he waved good-bye to the others and swung off down the street in the direction of the library.

Nan was curious to see Peggy's room and she and Helen and Peggy fell into easy conversation. As usual, the talk was of their dominant interest.

"In some ways I don't really welcome this vacation at all," Peggy said. "In the first place, *Peter Ibbetson* is not an easy play to do and the more we rehearse, the better it is likely to be. Quite aside from that, it is really no fun to have three days off with nothing specially to do in a strange town."

Suddenly it came to Nan how fortunate she was. The town was not so strange to her as it was to the others. She had friends outside the theater. Here was the time and the opportunity to give that luncheon that Mrs. Stockton had suggested so long ago! Of course, she'd have to ask first, but she was pretty sure it would be all right.

The afternoon passed pleasantly and at supper Nan asked her question.

"Do you remember, Aunt Peggy, that you suggested I bring a group from the company for luncheon some time? Well, with these three days off, quite a few of them are at loose ends. Might we plan a luncheon?"

Mrs. Stockton fell in with the idea eagerly and in the end it was decided that Wednesday was the best time, and they would ask Mark, Bud Parks, Peggy Worth, Helen Graves, Sally Holly and Alicia.

"And perhaps Roger Tyler might enjoy coming?" Mrs. Stockton proposed and Nan agreed. They purposely left Jud out, after some discussion. He was neither of the theater nor interested in it, as Roger was.

"Of course they may not all accept, especially Sally and Alicia," Nan said as she sat down to telephone the people they had selected for Wednesday's party. To her surprise and delight, they all accepted.

"If it is a hot day, we can take them out to the club afterwards for a swim," Mrs. Stockton had suggested, so Nan told everyone to bring a bathing suit.

That night, when she sat down to write to her mother, she was very contented. She wrote—

—I'm really beginning to think I *might*, with hard work, make a fair go of acting. Oddly enough, Alicia has helped me a lot. Why I don't know, but she has. I enjoy every minute of my time at the theater and I truly like the people. If it weren't for a luncheon party Aunt Peggy is giving, I'd really be bored with these days off.

I do miss you, Mother, and Grandmother too, but I know I have matured a lot this summer and that the old crowd would not hold the charm for me that it did before. I guess I am well on my way to being the Thespian you always had faith I would be.

26

Disaster Strikes

ON THE DAY OF THE LUNCHEON, Nan was surprised and a little put out when Mark arrived with Sally in her car. Nan clearly remembered that Sally had said she had made a mistake in dating Mark before, yet the other day she had driven him to the club to return the borrowed props, and here they were, together again.

Nan tried to greet them casually and cheerfully but Sally must have sensed her dismay, for she said, "See what I picked up on the street," and gestured toward Mark.

"Honked at me and got me, just like that!" Mark snapped his fingers, "I always was a pushover for a pretty girl in a convertible."

To Nan, it all seemed too elaborately explained, but as Helen Graves arrived just then, she put it out of her mind.

Roger came shortly afterwards, and since Petty Worth had come early, it left only Alicia still to arrive.

Nan knew that, in order to have time to go to the club for a swim before the evening performance, they would have to eat soon, so, as the time passed, she became more and more impatient.

"Why can't Alicia ever be on time?" she complained to Mark in a low tone.

"I'm afraid she suffers from a compulsion to call attention to herself."

"But, Mark, it's the wrong kind of attention. And she could so easily cultivate the right kind. I told her so only last week."

"You told her! Whew!"

"Yes, I know, it's funny. I have such a little bit of confidence in myself and I accused her of trying to cover up the same defect."

"By the way, I've been so busy all week, I haven't had a chance to ask you. How did you make out that day Alicia cued you? You never told me."

"Wonderfully, Mark. I really feel I could do the part now."

"Good!"

"Not that I'll have a chance to. Miss Dyke is the healthy type."

Mark laughed and just then Mrs. Stockton came up to them to suggest that they go in to luncheon and not wait any longer for Alicia.

The meal was a gay affair and everybody seemed to enjoy it. Afterwards, they gathered in the living room and listened to the record player. Quiet Roger turned out to be an expert on all forms of jazz, of which Mr. Stockton had quite a representative collection. Still no Alicia.

Mrs. Stockton finally called Alicia's hotel and was told that she had left there over an hour before.

"I do hope nothing has happened to her," she said.

"Oh, I don't think so. Alicia is not the reckless type," Mark assured her.

"Perhaps she mistook the date, or something of that sort," Nan suggested.

"She might be late, but I do not think she would be wholly discourteous," Mrs. Stockton said.

To Nan's surprise, it was Sally who promptly agreed with her. "You're right, Mrs. Stockton. I'm a lot like her, you know," she declared frankly, "but there are limits beyond which I do not believe either of us would go. Discourteous behavior to you is such a limit."

All of them agreed, however, that, no matter what the reason might be for Alicia's absence, there was nothing further they could do beyond having phoned the hotel, so they piled into three cars—Sally's, Roger's and the Stocktons'—and started for the club. Word was left with Annie to send Alicia out in a cab if she arrived.

The cool pool was welcomed by all of them and they would have thoroughly enjoyed the afternoon if it had not been for the disquiet which Alicia's absence imposed on them.

When the afternoon drew to a close, they were all warm in their thanks to Mrs. Stockton and to Nan. Roger and Sally elected to go straight home and the rest returned with Nan and Mrs. Stockton for a light repast before going to the theater.

Supper was almost over when the phone rang and Mrs. Stockton, who had left the dining room to answer it, came back looking white and shaken.

"That was Sally. She has just received word that Jud and Alicia were in a severe auto crack-up. They are both at the Metropolis Hospital and she's on her way there now."

"Oh, how terrible!" Nan was swept by a mixture of emotions.

"Why do you suppose she went out with Jud at all?" Helen asked.

"That's not important—though I think Sally is upset over

that question. I'll go down to the hospital myself and see about Alicia. Nan, do you know anything about her family? Who should be notified?"

"No, I don't, Aunt Peggy. She told me that her father and mother were divorced. I suppose Mr. Maguire has all that information."

"Mark, will you see that Joe Maguire knows about this? If he has not heard already."

"Yes, I will, of course."

It was a very sober group indeed that arrived at the theater.

Nan had a small part in *Seventh Heaven*, but when she reached her dressing room, Mr. Maguire and Hartley Bennett were there, waiting for her.

"Miss Dyke hasn't arrived and it's getting close to curtain time. We've not been able to reach her. You will have to go on."

Nan wanted to cry out, "I can't! Oh, I can't, not to-night, of all nights!" But she couldn't. This was the theater and she was the understudy. She would have to go on. Mechanically, she started to undress, but her thoughts were on a girl in a hospital bed who had once gone over this part with her.

How seriously was Alicia hurt?

27

The Show Must Go On

NAN WAS HELPED to dress and make up by the wardrobe mistress, something she had never experienced before. When she was ready, Mr. Bennett came into the dressing room and sat down.

"Would you like to go over the lines with me?" he asked, kindly.

"No, thanks. I think I do know them. What I am most worried over is the business."

"I'll keep an eye on you and the prompter will be on the job. It is too bad you didn't have time for even a brief walk-through. You're not nervous, are you?"

Nan laughed shakily. "I might have been if I'd had more time to think it over, but I'm more worried right now about my friend, Alicia Van Delyss. Did you know that she had been seriously hurt in an automobile accident this afternoon?"

"Yes, I heard. Too bad. I believe Mr. Maguire has gotten in touch with her people."

"Oh, I am glad of that!"

Mark's voice, outside the dressing room door, called, "Fifteen minutes to curtain."

"Mr. Bennett, could you please ask Mark to step in here

for a minute? Maybe he knows something further about Alicia."

Hartley Bennett rose, hesitated for a moment and then sat down again. "No, no," he said slowly. "You already know that all is being done for Miss Van Delyss that can be done. Tonight you are doing your first big part—*that* is all that you must think of now. Unless Miss Dyke arrives in the next few minutes, which seems unlikely, *you* are Diane in *Seventh Heaven*."

Wide-eyed, Nan looked at him and then said submissively, "Yes, Mr. Bennett."

"That's the spirit, girl. Now, let me see—a bit more eye-shade? Yes, I think so. Here—" He took up up the stick of eye-shade and he did not leave Nan until the call came, "Five minutes, on stage."

It was fortunate for Nan that she had learned her lines so scrupulously, for the ease with which they now came to her lips helped her over the first few minutes of panic. She felt that her voice tended to shake at first and was too high pitched, but within a short time, everything except the part she was playing was blotted out. Hartley Bennett gave her wonderful support and, when the curtain fell on the first act, she was surprised at the amount of applause.

Backstage, the cast congratulated her and told her to "keep it up," so it was a much more assured Nan who answered the second act curtain.

Though she did not know it until the play was over, a much distressed Lorna Dyke had arrived at the theater in the middle of the second act. She had been out of town with friends and they had run out of gas on a lonely stretch of road. By the time she could reach a telephone, the play had begun and by the time she reached the theater, Nan was well into the second act. Miss Dyke, upset as she was, nevertheless proved a very good sport about it. She sat down far in the back of the orchestra seats, where Nan would not see her and so be disturbed.

When the final curtain fell, there were three curtain calls, which for a mid-week, small "house" was not at all bad, Mr. Bennett assured Nan, as he held her hands warmly in congratulation.

She was standing surrounded by the cast when Mr. Murray and Miss Dyke came up to her.

"A very workmanlike job, my dear," Mr. Murray said.

Lorna Dyke kissed her and apologized all in one breath.

Suddenly Nan was ashamed to find that she had burst into tears.

It was Mr. Hanig who took her in a fatherly embrace.

"There, there. It's all over now and you did a good job. Go ahead and cry," he said comfortingly, patting her back.

"I—I'm sorry," Nan stammered, dabbing at her now streaked make-up. "I g-guess all of it was just too much for me. Did I do all right, really?"

"You did fine."

"Splendid!"

"O.K."

A smile broke through Nan's tears. "You're wonderful, all of you, and I'm so grateful—" She was threatening to break down again, so she made quickly for her dressing room, where the wardrobe mistress helped her once more.

Outside, Mark waited for her. When she saw him, Nan flew to him and, for the first time, he held her in his arms and kissed her tenderly.

"Nan, it was fine! You're quite an actress."

"Oh, Mark!" she raised sparkling eyes to his. "I *loved* doing it, even though I was so scared. Mark, I do believe I *am* going to be an actress!"

Mark smiled at her and then held her off and looked at her, his dark eyes sober, "Always?" he asked.

She knew what he meant and answered softly, "For a while, Mark."

"Right. We've time ahead for both of us to make good in."

"Mark, I was too excited to ask before. How is Alicia? And Jud?"

"Both pretty bad, I hear."

"Do you suppose I could go to see them?"

"Hardly at this hour! Tomorrow, perhaps. I'll take you home now."

"Mark, I'm so sorry that neither Aunt Peggy, nor Annie, —nor, of course, my own mother—were here this evening, but I suppose if they had been, it would only have made it harder for me."

"I tried to reach them on the phone the minute I heard that you were to go on, but Mrs. Stockton had left for the hospital, Annie said, and she didn't feel she could just walk out, without anyone to tell about it. She told me to tell you she'd be praying for you and I didn't even get a chance to do that! Anyway, I was here, and I'm glad of that, for now I know what a good actress my girl is." Mark squeezed her hand.

"Thank you. I'm awfully glad you were there, too," Nan answered softly.

Quietly, hand in hand, they walked to the bus together, and when they reached the Stockton house, Nan said, "Mark, don't come in tonight, do you mind? I'm so very tired right now."

"Of course you are, dear. I'll call you tomorrow."

Quite simply he kissed her again and Nan went on into the house to tell Mrs. Stockton what had happened to her.

When she has recounted events of the evening, Mrs. Stockton said, "That's a lot of emotion for one night, child. Yes, I went to the hospital. Alicia is not too badly hurt, though she has a broken arm, cuts and bruises. I'll drive you down tomorrow to see her. Meanwhile, get your rest tonight, and Nan—I hope you won't let success in the theater blind you to other things in life."

Nan wondered if Mrs. Stockton was alluding to Mark, though of that part of her evening she had said nothing, so now she answered shyly, "I won't Aunt Peggy, I promise you. I'll tell you now that Mark and I have—well, we have a sort of understanding about the future." A blush rose to her cheeks, but she went steadily on. "It will be years before we can think of marriage, of course. There is so much he wants to do, and I am going to try and make the kind of success my mother dreamed of for me. In the end though, what Mark and I really want is a home and a family."

"Good for you! He's a very fine boy and I'm glad for you, Nan. Now then, I'll get you some Ovaltine and you hop into your pajamas, and then, sleep for you."

Obediently, Nan prepared for bed, drank her Ovaltine, kissed Mrs. Stockton and got into bed. But she could not sleep. She lay staring into the darkness, longing for her mother.

Finally she got up, switched on the light and, crossing to the desk, drew out a sheet of notepaper and sat down to write.

Dearest Mother:
    It's late and I should be asleep, but I cannot sleep until I've talked with you. How I wish you were here tonight to talk to, face to face!
    Mother, when I came out here I told you that I was

not too sure I could be an actress. Now I know that I can. Tonight, I played the lead in *Seventh Heaven*. Of course I wasn't as good as Lorna Dyke, but everyone said I did very well and I really felt so myself. I know now that I can develop. I know now that I like the theater and the people in it better than anything else. It is all quite wonderful!

There is something else that I want you to know about, though you are not to worry over it.

I have grown very fond of Mark Byron, and, Mother, I do not think it is a childish affair. It may be years before we can get married. Mark wants to become a good director first and his ambition is to found a really good theater for children some time. I think maybe, by then, I will be glad to go into it with him. Meanwhile, we are very fond of each other and I wanted you to know about it.

The only bad thing I have to report is that Alicia was in a car accident yesterday with Jud Tompkins. I have not seen her yet, but will tomorrow. The theater has contacted her parents. No matter what happens to her, it seems she always puts her worst foot forward. She had an invitation to a luncheon party here at the Stocktons', together with some other friends of mine from the Company, and she apparently broke it to go driving with Jud.

Well, I guess I've unburdened myself enough to sleep! Please write and tell me that you are glad about Mark and me.

Your loving Thespian,

Nan

Nan sealed and stamped the envelope and, settling once more into bed, fell asleep almost immediately.

28

Explanations

THE FOLLOWING DAY, when Nan walked into the hospital room where Alicia lay, she was startled, not so much by the bandaged head and arm, but by the slow tears that squeezed their way from under Alicia's closed eyelids.

Involuntarily, Nan stopped short. The words of greeting about to pass her lips were choked back, and she stood, uncertain what to do. Instinctively, she knew Alicia would not like to be seen in this moment of weakness, yet if she were to leave now, she would surely reveal her presence. She cleared her throat tentatively, and as Alicia's eyes flew open, Nan put on a bit of an act. She was the breathless friend, bubbling with sympathy and questions, and she'd just that *moment* arrived. Nan wasn't sure it would fool Alicia, but it was worth a try.

"We were all so shocked, Alicia. I'd have been here last night, except that Miss Dyke never turned up and I had to do her part."

"How wonderful, Nan! How did it go?" Alicia looked really pleased.

"It went all right, I guess." Nan was suddenly shy. "But I didn't come here to talk about me, Alicia. How are you? Aunt Peggy said the worst was your arm—?"

164

"It was sweet of her to come right over yesterday—especially after the way I went off with Jud, with never a word of explanation. I suppose everyone thought it was just like me?" The old hard tone was back in her voice.

"As a matter of fact, no. Sally said she just couldn't imagine you being really rude where it counted—" Nan stopped abruptly, realizing she had gone too far.

"Nice of her! She knows me pretty well." Alicia sounded bitter.

"I didn't say that right, Alicia. Sally said she was a lot like you, but she didn't think either of you capable of pure bad manners."

"Where it counted?"

"She didn't say that," Nan denied miserably. "I did."

An uncomfortable silence fell, which Nan broke by asking once more how badly Alicia was injured.

"Not badly. The doctors say I may have a slight scar on my forehead, where my head hit the dashboard, and my arm is broken. I'll be out of here in a few days, though; but I doubt if I'll return to the company."

"Why not?" Nan was surprised.

Alicia turned her head restlessly on the pillow. Nan could not tell whether she was in pain or not but she seemed to want to talk so Nan let her.

"Both my parents are on the way out here now and, if I know them, they'll make this the occasion for seeing that I get sent away to school again, or for a trip, if I can talk them into that. I threw quite a few tantrums to get them to consent to my taking this job. They won't like this mess a bit."

"Alicia why did you do it? Go with Jud, I mean?"

"You won't believe me, Nan, I know, but I never meant to. When I left the hotel to go to your house, Jud was outside in his car, and he offered to drive me to wherever I was going. I told him I was going to your house and he said O.K. He never let on that he already knew about the luncheon and that he hadn't been invited, so, of course, I got into the car. I don't know Metropolis very well, so it was quite a while before I guessed we weren't headed for the Stocktons' place at all."

Alicia stopped and shuddered slightly.

"Don't tell me about it, if it upsets you," Nan urged, though she was dying to hear the whole story.

"No, I want you to know. I realized pretty soon that Jud had had something to drink. I'd never seen him like that before and it scared me. I may sometimes act as if I was very sophisticated, but Nan, I never could stand drinking! That awful Mr. Torley was always asking me to have just a little drink. It is why I stopped going out with him. Anyway, it was dreadful! Jud said he wanted to marry me. He said Sally had jilted him and that he was desperate. He said he'd do anything for me, just so he wouldn't be a laughing stock because Sally had turned him down. Naturally, I argued. I told him Sally was a wonderful girl and I didn't think she cared for anyone but him, but that she had to get the theater out of her system first. Then he brought Mark in. Said Sally had fallen for him and I said, no she hadn't. It went on that way, mile after mile. Once we stopped at a roadhouse and Jud ordered a drink. I didn't take a thing. By then I was afraid he'd do something crazy and I figured maybe I'd better stick by him and do most anything he wanted until he came to his senses. It was about then that the accident happened. The funny part of it was Jud wasn't really at fault. Matter of fact, he swerved to avoid hitting a little girl that ran into the street and then he rammed right into a tree." Alicia stopped speaking and then added, wearily, "so that's it. Not that I expect to be believed."

Nan, remembering Jud's conversation with her in front of the theater and his unwavering belief in his own ideas, as well as his intense jealousy, said simply, "But I do believe you, Alicia. It's just like Jud. I'm awfully sorry it happened, of course, but I'm glad it wasn't your fault. I hear Jud is pretty badly hurt, but Sally has been with him and perhaps they'll straighten things out. It's you I'm worried about, though. Mrs. Stockton told me to ask you if you could come and stay with us when you get out of here—that is, if your parents will consent. There are several extra guest rooms and you could keep more in touch with things at the theater, having me there, too."

Alicia's face lit up. "Did she honestly invite me, Nan?" she asked.

"Honestly," Nan said and watched the incredible hazel eyes fill and overflow.

Mrs. Stockton's warmly tendered, impulsive invitation to a girl in trouble did much to soothe Alicia's parents on their arrival in Metropolis. They had arrived and taken up their separate abodes, at different hotels. Their mutual concern for their child was relieved considerably by Mrs. Stockton's offer.

Due to the pressure of business, Alicia's father left first for the East, while her mother lingered a little longer, until Alicia was discharged from the hospital and settled at the Stocktons'.

The day had come, however, for Mrs. Van Delyss' own departure and she was saying her good-byes to Mrs. Stockton.

"I don't know how much I can thank you for being so kind to my dear little girl. Your taking her in has quite avoided the scandal her own rash actions brought about."

Alicia and Nan looked uncomfortable, but Mrs. Stockton replied briskly. "I don't think there was any thought of scandal involved. In any case, I've grown very fond of your daughter, Mrs. Van Delyss. It is fine for Nan to have her here, too. I hate to hurry you, but your train—"

"Goodness yes! Good-bye, Alicia. Good-bye, Nan." Fluttering, talking, gesturing, Mrs. Van Delyss hurried down the walk and into the car, to be driven to the station by Mrs. Stockton.

Slowly the two girls reentered the house.

"Oh, Nan," Alicia said, "I wish I could like my father and mother better. Father *is* a bit of a pet, but mother is apt to be impossible. I don't think she's really concerned with anyone but herself and what people will think of her." Suddenly Alicia stopped and, in a surprised tone of discovery, added, "I guess I'm a lot like her."

Nan nodded. "You could be, easily. But Alicia, you've another side to you, if you'd let it grow. Look how nice you've been to me. Oh, I know at first you thought I had some influence—connections that counted. Actually though, it wasn't only this that made you friendly to me, was it?"

"Well, no."

"What then? I have always wondered. At first I was annoyed by you—by your aloofness and your air of calculation. But even then I was kind of shocked by it, too. It seems to me I wouldn't have been shocked if that's the way you really were. It was like seeing you do a poor piece of acting—as if the only character you never really figured out was yourself." Nan stooped, wondering how the new and quieter Alicia would take this frankness.

In the week just past, Alicia had shown herself to be

intelligent, full of unexpected fun, and, except when her mother had been with them, she had seemed relaxed and happy. Nan waited anxiously.

When Alicia spoke it was slowly, thoughtfully, and with honesty.

"I'm glad you uncovered that 'me' which I came close to burying, Nan. You see, ever since my parents' divorce, I've felt as though no one really wanted me. No, not even Dad. I knew I had talent and it was so easy to put on an act and get what I wanted from my parents. I came to feel that anything I wanted could be had in the same way. I was cynical about people. Then I met you. You seemed so simple—simple-minded, I thought at first. Later I realized you were much more secure than I was. Certainly, you knew the right people, but, if anything, you pushed them off. You stood on your own feet, and yet, like my coaching, you were grateful for help, if you felt you needed it. I admired your calm. I even admired your calm when Sally made such a set for Mark."

Nan laughed. "I wasn't a bit calm inside about that! But I did trust Mark, deep down, I think."

"That's it! You trust people. It's what I have to learn to do. Once you trust people, you can like them. You're not afraid. Well, it may be too late, but I'm going to try for the rest of the season."

"Good for you!"

"Do you suppose the doctor will let me go back to rehearsals next week?"

"I think so."

"Nan, if he does, will you kick me or something if you see me acting the way I did before?"

"Gladly!" Nan exclaimed so heartily that they both laughed.

"There is one thing that really bothers me, though," Alicia continued, "and that is Sally. Mrs. Stockton says Jud is still in the hospital and may be there for some time. I don't know what he told Sally about that day, but the fact remains that she never got in touch with me. If you find a chance, will you try to tell her I didn't plan to go with Jud that day?"

"I'd love to tell her! But she hasn't turned up at the theater since the accident. I can't understand her myself. It doesn't seem like her not to even ask about you. But I'll try to give her the real story the first time I see her—and that will positively be my last good deed for the season!"

Again they laughed and together began the task of dressing Alicia for an appointment with the doctor.

Nan could not help wondering if much of the ease with which she and Alicia now talked to each other was not due to Alicia's need for help in dressing herself, with the cast on her arm. It would be difficult, at best, to remain aloof while someone buttoned you up, like a small girl in a pinafore. At any rate, Alicia was now a friend, and for this Nan was glad.

29

Now I Know

SEVENTH HEAVEN played out a second week and then *Peter Ibbetson* was produced.

Of all the plays that were given that season, *Peter Ibbetson* was to leave the deepest impression on Nan.

To begin with, it was a tragedy and a much more deeply realized one than *Smilin' Through*. At leads they had, to Nan's intense surprise and delight, Edith Trevor and Shawn Glynn—surely two of the finest stars that even Broadway could ask for.

Nan wondered if Miss Trevor would remember her and suffered a return of "butterflies" in her stomach, as Annie had described it, on the day the great actress was to arrive.

Nan need not have worried, however, for Miss Trevor saw her across the greenroom, nodded pleasantly, and, after the reading was through, she walked directly over to Nan.

"Hello, Nan," she said easily, "I was asking about you and I hear you've done very well."

"Oh, Miss Trevor, thank you! It has been a wonderful season and I think I've found myself."

"You want to act then?"

"Yes, I do. I'm sure now. Unless—I mean, if I *should* get married, I feel that would be my real career."

Miss Trevor smiled. "It's a woman's first career, always. I left the stage for quite a while when my children were small."

Nan stammered, "I—I didn't know you had children."

"Yes, I have two—a boy and a girl. Both are in college now. Some time I'll show you their pictures. Well, Nan, I'm glad the season has helped you to make up your mind and still not lose your honesty."

"I hate to see it end," Nan said, "but no ending could be better than having the opportunity to watch you rehearse."

"Thank you. I'll see you around then."

Nan nodded and Miss Trevor went off. Immediately Nan was surrounded by her friends.

"I didn't know you knew her," Bud said.

"What's she like? I've never seen her act, but I've heard so much about her," Helen Graves added.

Nan saw Alicia, on the fringe of the group, her arm still in a sling and the old hard expression in her eyes.

"I don't really know her," Nan said and looked directly at Alicia. "One night, in New York, a friend of my mother's introduced me to Miss Trevor—I never in the world thought she'd remember me! And do you know *why* she did?"

They waited.

"She remembered me because I was such a mixed-up kid that I blurted out to her, of all people, that I wasn't sure I wanted to be an actress!"

They laughed and Bud queried, "Well, do you now?"

"Miss Trevor said this summer would give me the chance to really find out—and it has. Yes, I want to act."

"How did this summer help you to decide?" Bud asked.

"For one thing, I had the opportunity of watching really good acting and directing; for another, I found that theater people are pretty swell. I learned a lot from all of you and especially from Alicia, and I'm grateful."

Naturally, everyone turned to look at Alicia and if they were surprised to see her blush, Nan was not. However, she turned the compliment aside neatly. "That's right, I'm the greatest coach of the century. For a small fee, I'll coach anyone. Any takers?"

The moment of seriousness blew over on a laugh, but Nan was glad of that moment, for it showed how far Alicia had come and that the company were beginning to accept her.

The week of rehearsals for *Peter Ibbetson* was fraught with emotion, for Shawn Glynn was so overcome by the part that he actually broke down in rehearsal and cried on-stage. Half the cast found themselves with wet eyes. Yet Bud and Alicia both thought that he would do a better job when he was less emotional about it.

And so it proved, for by the time the play was put on, he could simulate what he had previously experienced, and his voice became a more reliable instrument for conveying emotion.

Peter Ibbetson was the last play of the season, and they would give it for two weeks. During the last week, Mrs. Stockton planned her annual luncheon for the entire cast of the stock company. In this Alicia was a great help, for she now had more time free than Nan.

One evening, when Nan arrived home, she found the two of them discussing Sally.

"Jud is out of the hospital now, but still Sally has not contacted any of us," Alicia was saying.

"We were wondering whether to invite Sally to the party or not," Mrs. Stockton explained to Nan.

"I'll stay home, if she'd rather not meet me," Alicia offered, for the luncheon was to be held at the club.

"Indeed you won't!" both Mrs. Stockton and Nan protested.

Alicia looked pleased, but asked, "What then?"

"I'll go and see Sally tomorrow," Nan asserted with decision. "I've promised I would and I never have, because it's an unpleasant task; but it's time she knew the truth about that accident. . . . Besides, I'm curious," she added frankly.

30

Matters Are Cleared Up

WHEN NAN CALLED SALLY the following day she received an evasive reply at first, but she was insistent.

"Sally, I simply *must* see you," she declared. "It concerns more than just you. After all, not so long ago, the theater meant everything to you and you were so grateful to me— or so you said."

It was an unfair advantage, perhaps, but Nan was determined that Sally would see her.

"All right. I'll meet you at the hotel for lunch," Sally agreed.

Nan was not prepared for the Sally who came into the hotel lobby. She was thin and she looked actually sick.

After they had gone into the dining room and ordered their meal, Nan came directly to the point.

"Sally, Mrs. Stockton is giving her usual luncheon for the cast out at the club this week. The question of asking you came up and Alicia offered to stay home, if you'd come, but we both said no. Sally, what did Jud tell you about the accident?"

"He said Alicia didn't want to go to the party at your place. He said they made the date to go out and that they'd both been drinking. He said he'd done it to spite me. She's no good and Jud was almost killed."

Pityingly, Nan looked at Sally. Even though she believed Jud, she did not look happy.

"Sally," Nan said gently, "not one word of that is true, except that Jud did nearly kill them both." Quietly then, she told Sally the truth and ended, "If you don't believe me, the hospital can tell you. Alicia had not been drinking at all, but Jud had."

Sally covered her face with her hands.

"Alicia is a different person now, Sally, and she'd like you to understand."

"I guess I suspected it all along. Jud uses the whole episode as a club over me. He almost got me to promise not to enter dramatic school this fall, but I didn't quite give in on that. It's nice not to have to hate anyone. I just feel sorry for Jud."

"Will you come to the luncheon then?"

"No, though I think Mrs. Stockton, and you too, Nan, are sweet to ask me. I've never been a real member of the company, I'd feel awkward attending right now. Besides, it might get back to Jud. He's still pretty sick. No, I'll not hurt him deliberately now. Then when I do go to dramatic school, he will have time to grow up, or we will drift apart. Tell Alicia I'm sorry I misjudged her, and I'm thankful she wasn't more seriously hurt."

During the rest of the meal, the two talked about the stage and Sally asked a million questions about the cast and Edith Trevor. Knowing how much it would have meant to Sally to have had the opportunity of observing such an actress at work, Nan could not but admire her fortitude in foregoing it for Jud's sake. She strongly suspected that in the end Jud would realize that Sally could love both him and the theater. She had given every proof of it already, it seemed to Nan.

When she reached home, Nan was happy to be able to tell Alicia that, at last, Sally understood what had really happened and even more happy when a short note arrived from Sally to Alicia.

In it Sally asked Alicia's forgiveness and explained her misunderstanding. She ended by saying that she had about decided to enter the Booth School in the fall and that she hoped during the following winter she and Alicia and Nan could be together sometimes.

Handing the note to Nan to read, Alicia waited until she had finished it and then remarked, "I almost wish I were going back to school myself. Perhaps I'd get more out of it now. However, it is life, real life, in earnest for me. Oh, Nan, do you suppose I can land a job?"

"I should think you'd stand a good chance. You have your fine experience this summer to show and you were mentioned favorably in several reviews."

It gave Nan an odd feeling to be reassuring the confident Alicia!

The End and the Beginning

THE LUNCHEON PARTY at the club was a great success and everyone seemed to enjoy it thoroughly.

Nan was particularly amazed and delighted by the lighthearted playfulness of the stars, of whom she and the rest of the cast always stood in some awe. Miss Trevor did an imitation of a currently popular "blues" singer which brought the house down, and Mr. Bennett, not to be outdone, did a take-off on Mr. Murray himself, which reduced that usually very tense man to helpless tears of laughter.

There remained but two days more of the stock company's season, when a notice appeared on the bulletin board.

ENTIRE CAST REPORT AT 3 P.M. FRIDAY

Neither Nan nor Alicia had any idea as to why they were called, since there was no new play to be read.

It was with the greatest curiosity then that the two girls reported to the greenroom on Friday, to find it already filled. Under the window ledge, where Nan had sat so often, there was a long table, with a punch bowl, glasses and many small sandwiches and petits-fours.

"A party!" Nan exclaimed happily.

Mark saw them and came over.

"Is this a custom?" Alicia asked.

"Yes, or so Joe Maguire says. It seems Professor Murray takes over here and gives a small lecture before the party."

Nan giggled and explained to Alicia, "Mr. Murray was a teacher once."

"Wonder what he'll talk about?" Alicia questioned curiously.

"*Sssh!* He's going to start now."

Mark, Nan and Alicia linked arms and stood where they were.

It was a brief resumé of the highlights of the past season, including an account of the business they had done at the box office. It was all quite informal and Mr. Murray made special mention of Miss Fair and her bravery, "in the best tradition of the theater," in continuing her role after she became ill. They all applauded that. He mentioned, too, the current production of *Peter Ibbetson*, "which has given the theatergoers of Metropolis an experience they'll long remember."

Spontaneously, the applause broke out again. When it stopped, Mr. Murray went on.

"It is my yearly custom to make special mention of the students and newcomers to our company, in the hopes that what I say may be helpful to them in the future."

From here he went on to each individual boy or girl, giving a brief word of encouragement or criticism.

Nan could hardly wait to hear what he would say about her.

At last her turn came.

"Nan Lane is the youngest member of our company this year. She will have to work on her voice, which has the thin quality of youth. However, I like her work and especially her attitude toward it." He turned to address Nan directly. "I believe you will make the grade and I wish you luck."

Nan could have danced with joy. It was praise from the person who counted most.

Of Alicia he said, "Miss Van Delyss, a new member of the company, has had an unfortunate year, due to her accident. However, she has great talent and I am happy to offer her a contract with us for next summer, if she so desires."

To Nan's delight, there was applause and she squeezed Alicia's arm tightly.

When the speechmaking was over, there was a general rush for the table and soon, refreshments in hand, everyone was busily chatting.

As Nan finished the food Mark had brought her, he said quietly, "Nan, slip out into the theater with me for a minute, will you?"

Nan nodded agreement and followed him.

No longer was the shadowy interior, with its red EXIT lights, strange to her. It seemed long ago that Mark had held her hand and led her through this same theater.

Quietly Nan sat down beside him in one of the orchestra seats, as she once had sat beside Sally.

"Nan," Mark began abruptly, "I'm not going back to school."

Nan's heart stood still and all her world seemed to crash about her. Why, why, when she was so very happy? The cry escaped her lips, soft as a breath, "*Why?*"

"Because I've been offered a good job as an assistant stage manager on Broadway. Because I'm not interested in acting for myself. I feel I can learn as much, or more, by this actual experience, but most of all, Nan, because I don't want to wait too long to establish myself until I can ask you to be my wife. You're going to be an actress—and a good one—but, Nan, will you hold me in your heart?" He reached for her hands and held them both cupped in his strong ones.

"You are already there, Mark," Nan answered surely and simply.

Hands clasped in the darkness, Nan could feel the beating of her heart, that heart which was all Mark's. He would be in New York. They would see each other. They would both work hard.

Mark finally broke the silence. "Perhaps one day I *can* direct my own star," he said and leaned over to kiss her.

As he released her and stood up that they might return to the others, Nan laughed shakily.

"I guess I have grown up more than Mr. Murray thinks," she said.

"We've both grown up, this summer in stock," Mark answered soberly, as they made their way toward the greenroom.

ABOUT THE AUTHOR

Kathleen S. Tiffany was born in Tennessee and brought up in New York City. She attended school in Alabama, dramatic school in New York and studied dancing in France and England. She acted briefly, professionally, before her marriage at seventeen. After leaving the stage, she became a librarian, specializing in work with children, where her early dramatic training has found a place in puppetry. At present she is a librarian in The New York Public Library, where she has had most of her professional experience.

The author says that she has "enjoyed writing since my earliest years." When the *Dodd, Mead Librarian Prize Competition* originated, she entered her charming first book, *Mary Florence*, in the contest and won a well-deserved Honorable Mention Award for this genuine piece of Americana. The story is based on rich reminiscences passed on to her first hand by an old lady who actually heard Abraham Lincoln's Gettysburg address.

Kathleen S. Tiffany says: "I have one married son, and I am interested in children, my church, books, swimming, sailing, stamps, dogs and baseball!"

5507